THE DRAGON'S PROPHECY

LILY WINTER

D1522221

WHITE HAT PRESS

COPYRIGHT

The Dragon's Prophecy
Immortal Dragon, Book 6
Copyright © 2020 by Lily Winter
Cover Artist: The Book Brander
Edited by: Red Adept Editing

OTHER TITLES BY LILY WINTER

Fated Mates of the Underworld
Banished Wolf
Claimed Witch
Exiled Demigod
Immortal Dragon
The Dragon's Psychic
The Dragon's Human
The Dragon's Mate
The Dragon's Hunt
The Dragon's Wolf
The Dragon's Prophecy

ROMANTIC SUSPENSE BOOKS BY LINZI BAXTER

Lily's alter ego

White Hat Security Series
Hacker reExposed
Royal Hacker
Misunderstood Hacker
Undercover Hacker
Hacker Revelation
Hacker Christmas
Hacker Salvation
Hacker Enclosed
Hacker Wedding - Jan 12, 2021
Nova Satellite Security Series
(White Hat Security Spin Off)

Pursuing Phoenix

Pursuing Aries

Pursuing Pegasus

Pursuing Columbia Mar 30, 2021

Pursuing Cygnus May 25, 2021

A Flipping Love Story (Special Forces World)

Unlocking Dreams

Unlocking Hope

Unlocking Love

Unlocking Desire

Unlocking Secrets Apr 27, 2021

Unlocking Lies

Montana Gold (Brotherhood Protector World)

Grayson's Angel

Noah's Love

Bryson's Treasure

Visit linzibaxter.com for more information and release dates.

Join Linzi Baxter Newsletter at Newsletter

ALIDA

*A*lida Zayvrus counted to ten as she followed her dad up the stairs. On the car ride to DC, he'd talked about how he worried she would accidentally use her powers at college, but he was the one making a fire-clicking noise in the back of his throat.

Her parents, Kirin and Talia, had insisted on driving to college to help her move into the dorms. For a second, she'd contemplated transporting her things back and forth with her powers, but they'd quickly shot down that idea. Her roommate was human, after all.

Ninety-five percent of the people at her new college were human. Alida worried a little about slipping and using her powers accidentally. College wasn't her first time in the actual world, but it was the first time she would be completely surrounded by humans. Growing up, she'd gone to a shifter school, then she'd earned her bachelor's at a four-year college close to home. Now she was working on her master's. Most of her friends were shifters who had chosen not to go to college and to work for her dad at the council.

Alida wanted to branch out, though. Her parents had talked her into staying close to home for the first four years of college. In the beginning, she'd tried to move away then decided against it. But now she felt a powerful pull to move to DC.

. "Dad, you promised to act normal," she murmured.

Her family was far from ordinary. She loved her little brother and sister, but she was glad they hadn't come on this road trip. It was the first actual road trip they had ever taken. In the past, she'd always transported them wherever they needed to go. They'd only spent time in shifter communities when on vacation.

"He's trying," her mother said as she placed her gloved hand on Alida's back. All they needed was for her mom to accidentally touch one of her classmates and see that person's past. Alida only hoped no one commented on the white gloves, because that would cause her dad to growl even more.

She could have come to college on her own. It wasn't like she was eighteen and moving out. No, she was twenty-two years old. But they'd both insisted, saying most parents helped their kids move to college. She'd given up on pointing out that they weren't most families.

Alida knew her dad had plans to make one last-ditch effort to convince her to come home and finish school locally.

Kirin opened the door at the top of the stairs. College kids and their parents filled the hallway. Alida caught a few arguing about being okay. She closed off her mind so she didn't start reading everyone's thoughts. When she was younger, controlling all of her powers had been hard, but now she had a grasp on most. Sometimes it was still hard to control her temper, and things might fly across the room.

The people filling the hall parted like the Red Sea as her dad walked down the center. To her, he was a big old teddy bear—well, a dragon—but most ran in the other direction. Her dorm room was only two down from the main stairwell. She shifted the box to her other hand and opened the door.

Her home for the next ten months, it was a lot smaller than her bedroom at her parents' house. At home, she had an entire wing to herself, including a small kitchen and game room. Now she was about to share a room smaller than her closet with someone else. And she couldn't have been more excited.

Talia lowered her box to the twin bed and spun in a circle, not saying a word. Alida contemplated going into her mom's mind for a second and listing to her thoughts, but she tried not to do that. Sometimes, she found her mother thinking dirty things about her dad, and she would end up gagging. Talia always said it served her right for reading her mind.

Kirin was the last to set his box down on the bed and glance around the white-brick-walled room. The bricks looked similar to the ugly beige ones used in the prison below the council building. The lighting in her room was better than the prison, though, and it came with a view of the main quad area.

"Well, this is better than I thought," he mumbled as he pulled Talia next to him.

"It's bigger than the home you grew up in," Talia said as she pressed a hand to Kirin's chest and smiled up at him.

Alida loved how much her parents cared about each other. She'd seen true love twice—once with the parents who'd raised her until she was eight and again with her adopted parents, Kirin and Talia. It wasn't until after Kirin and Talia had adopted her that she'd found out her original dad had made her in a test tube. That was how she'd ended up with so many powers nobody understood. Kirin worked hard with his brothers to shut down those projects and close the labs. Every so often, someone would try to recreate the formula, but nobody had succeeded in years, and she was happy about that.

She would miss her parents. They were only trying to protect her from most of the world, even though she was an adult. And her dad didn't want her taking any high-risk positions with the council because he worried something might happen to her. But Alida wished to be by his side and help him run everything.

Going off to college was proof she could be on her own.

Kirin worried she wouldn't be able to protect herself if someone came after her. That was insane, though, since she had more powers than she under-stood—and she could transport. In the past five years, not one person had threatened her life. Her savant uncle always kept searches on her name, so they knew if someone planned to come after her powers.

Alida turned her attention from the window to her father. He was a foot taller than her five foot five. She always had to look up when talking to him. "You lived in a small house?"

Kirin nodded. "When I was a kid, your uncles and I lived in a small two-bed cabin."

She couldn't help but roll her eyes. Kirin and her uncles had been babies over three hundred years ago. Of course, the place he'd lived in back then was small.

"Are you guys heading back home now?"

For a second, she didn't want her parents to leave. Over the past thirteen years, she hadn't been away from them for more than a couple of days. Now, they would be apart for a long time. She wanted to spend a few more hours with them before they headed out.

"I think we are going to spend a couple nights in town and maybe head to Florida for a week. Candace and Kayda wanted to spend some time at the beach."

Fog floated through Alida's mind. That happened every time she was about to see the future. She didn't choose what glimpse of the future she would get; they just appeared. Some visions came in clearly, and some were objects she wouldn't understand until other visions came. And now, a vision came over her: Candace holding two cute little baby boys. The fog cleared, and both of her parents were staring at her, waiting for her to tell them what she'd seen.

"Please tell me you didn't have a vision about Candace," her mother begged.

It wasn't her first vision about the human mated to a wolf shifter. Nope, she'd seen all eight of Candace's previous pregnancies. Now she was going to have twins. "Tell Candace congrats on the two little boys."

"Nope," her father growled.

"Are you sure, dear? That poor woman already has enough. You're telling me she is pregnant with twins?" Talia asked. "I might have to agree with your dad on this one. Some of your visions are better left unsaid. I'll let the local pack doctor explain she's having twins. No way in hell I'm going down that path."

Kirin turned and opened one of her boxes. "This is from Uncle Kai. Something about your old laptop not being good enough, and he added a bunch of things. I have no clue what they mean."

He'd probably also installed some way to track her internet history to make sure she was okay. Years ago, he'd put a tracker in her necklace. To this day, she didn't mind—it gave her some sense of security.

"I'll send him a thank-you text later."

The door to her dorm room opened, and a tall woman walked in, dressed from head to toe in black. In the center of her chest was a large red anarchy symbol. Alida did not expect that to go over well with her parents.

Behind the woman, a couple walked in, dressed in their Sunday best. They were the total opposite of their daughter.

"Hi, I'm Alida." She held out her hand.

As her new roommate reached out her hand, silver chains clicked around her wrist, and her black fingernails dug into Alida's skin a little as they shook. "I go by Raven."

Behind Raven, the older woman rolled her eyes and stepped forward. "I'm Patty's mother, Becca, and this is Richard."

Talia and Kirin introduced themselves and talked for a few more minutes while Raven emptied her first box. She spread a black blanket over her bed and placed a skull on the end table.

Alida wanted to scream when her mother removed her gloves and picked up the skull. She turned so nobody could see her eyes turn white while she read the object. Raven wasn't the only odd character in the room. Talia sat the skull back down and placed her gloves back on. "That is almost lifelike."

Raven shrugged and hung a picture of a warlock on the wall. Alida hadn't seen him in years.

How the hell did she get a photo of Kael? He was one of

the most corrupt men in the world. Before her parents could rip her out of the room, Alida let the hold on her powers go a smidge. "That is the coolest photo. Who is that?"

"There's a dark legend he was the most powerful warlock, and he's waiting to come back. Haven't you seen the new movie about him?"

Kirin growled, but Talia placed her hand on his chest.

"So, you do magic?"

Alida opened her mind to hear the woman's thoughts.

'How did I get stuck with the craziest roommate who would actually think magic is real?' Raven rolled her eyes. "Yep, and I plan to find a cult to follow."

Raven's mom pressed her hand to her lips, and a tiny tear fell from her eye. Alida didn't know the reason, but Raven was a bitch to her parents. With a little flick of Alida's finger, the skull flew off the table and crashed to the floor. And the sound of it cracking made her smile.

"How strange," Alida commented, squatting to pick up the little pieces of plastic.

Her father's thoughts rushed through her mind. 'No powers.' Even the idea came to her with his growl.

She shrugged and stood. "Well, I'm going to get lunch with my parents. See you later."

Alida wanted to experience every aspect of college, but maybe living off campus was more in her cards.

Or things could change once her roommate's parents left.

"Nice meeting you guys," Talia said as they walked out the door.

Kirin just nodded and pushed them into the hallway. Alida knew he would have a million questions for her and probably demand she come home, but that would not happen every time they sensed the smallest amount of danger.

Once outside the room, she pressed the door closed. "Don't worry. She doesn't believe any of it. She's doing it to piss off her parents."

"I can't believe there are pictures of Kael," her dad gritted out. "Or a fucking movie."

"Yeah, well, you know most of the legends in the magical world get made into a film," Talia said. "Kai could do some research if one got made about Kael. The skull, she bought before coming here, and Alida is right. She doesn't believe any of it. She's only doing it to make her parents mad."

Alida tried to hear into the room, but nobody was saying a word. She really wanted to know why her roommate hated her family.

Her dad sighed and ran his hand through his hair. "Since there is no chance in me talking you into heading back with us, do you think you will let me buy you a steak?"

"Yep." She might not have been a shifter like her dad, but that didn't mean she didn't eat like shifters.

Her metabolism was just as high as her dad's. And a large steak sounded good.

"Since I'm a poor college student, you're buying."

"I almost forgot." Kirin reached into his pocket and pulled out a credit card. "This is for you to buy what you need."

She was about to say thank you when laughter and shouting erupted in the hall. Everyone parted and backed up against the wall. Like they had when Kirin first walked down the hallway, everyone got out of the way.

The people weren't moving for him this time, though. A tall naked man with long, shaggy hair ran through the crowds. Someone shouted, "Streaker." His dick swung with each step he took.

He looked over his shoulder and cussed. Alida tried to stand on her tiptoes to see who he was running from, but she couldn't see. The naked man pumped his arms and ran faster, but he had on socks, making it hard for him not to slip with each step.

Her dad shook his head, and her mom laughed. Talia even cheered him on as he ran by, but Alida's eyes weren't on the naked man with a firm ass anymore. Nope, a taller man with short black hair was following the man.

He was only a few steps away from her when their eyes connected. The world around her hushed. She didn't have to work to keep the walls up—everything was quiet when she looked into his dark-blue eyes. It reminded her of the clouds on a rainy day.

The spell between them was broken when he lunged forward, swiping at the naked man's feet. She stepped into the center of the hall to watch as he wrestled the man and slipped a pair of plastic ties around his wrists.

He stood, hauling the naked man up, and she wanted to reach out and touch him.

The sexy man glared at her. "Can you move out of the center of the hall?"

And just like that, the spell was broken, and she couldn't figure out how he hadn't felt it too.

2

GRADY

"You ou need to make sure my grandson takes one of these each day," the elderly lady said as she tried to push a pill bottle into Grady's hand.

God, he hated move-in day. *Same shit, different year.*

"We don't make sure students take their meds," Grady sighed. At least she wasn't asking for his phone number, like the last three parents who'd knocked on his door. He couldn't understand why parents cared so much. Maybe it was because he'd never had parents or a loving mother. Years of foster care had left him to be bitter, also broke. The RA job helped pay for his college.

"Did you hear me? My poor boy will die if he doesn't take these pills at eight a.m. every morning." She tried pushing her way into his room. For a small old lady, she was strong. That still didn't mean he would make sure her grandson took his pills each morning. He barely remembered to take his own vitamins. No way would he remember someone else's.

Plus, it wasn't his job. A pamphlet given to each student outlined the RA's duties, but she refused to look at it.

"If you're worried about your grandson dying, maybe he's not ready for college," he mumbled, staring down at the old lady. Grady had a million other things he would rather do. Talking to a grandmother about her grandson's meds was not one of them. Spending the day watching Netflix before classes started was high on his list, not arguing with parents and the occasional grandmother.

"Grandmother!" A short nerdy boy came running, pushing his black rim glasses up as he came to a stop. "What are you doing?"

She cocked her head to the side. "Trying to get this stubborn man to take your meds. He needs to make sure you take them. Remember last year, the one day you forgot, and I came home, and you were on the ground. Who's going to make sure you're not dead?"

The nerdy guy's face turned as red as his Big Bang shirt. Grady guessed there was actually more to the story, but he didn't care. He just wanted them out of his doorway so he could go back to watching Netflix.

"Leave him alone, Grandmother." The kid sighed. "Remember, I have the cool app to help remind me?"

"How do I know that phone thing will go off properly? You young people put way too much faith in technology. In my day, neighbors helped each other out." She turned and glared at Grady, who would not bend to what she wanted.

"Can I have some help please?" another student yelled down the hall. "My roommate's lighting weeds in our room."

Having found an excuse to escape the old lady, he shut his door and walked down the corridor toward the young man who was complaining. When he walked by Room 1111, his feet stumbled for a second. Shaking his head, he continued down the hall until he was next to the man pointing in his room.

"Tell him to stop," the chubby freshman whined.

Grady walked into the room and stopped. He expected the guy to have lit a joint, not sage. He wasn't the first student who'd used sage to cleanse their space, though, and Grady suspected he wouldn't be the last.

"He's not doing anything wrong." Grady pinched the bridge of his nose. "The smell will be gone in a few minutes."

"But I have asthma," the freshman wheezed as he pulled out his inhaler and stuck it in Grady's face.

"You can always fill out a form to transfer rooms," he explained.

The young man finished dousing the room in sage and put away his things. It wasn't like the place even smelled anymore. Grady kept telling himself he only had two more semesters before he was done with college.

Grady turned as someone tapped him on the shoulder. "Can you please help me get my door unlocked?"

"Okay." He turned back to the original guy. "If you want to transfer, fill the form out online."

The man just stared.

Grady shrugged and followed the girl down the hall toward Room 1111 again. He felt a strange pull every time he passed the room. The freshman stopped outside the door to the room across from 1111. She put her key in the door, and nothing happened.

God, I hate move-in day. Grady closed his eyes and counted to five. "Are you sure this is your room?"

"I'm not sure. Everything is so overwhelming." She took a step forward and ran her finger along his arm. His first year as a RA, he would have taken the coed up on her offer. But now, his only mission was to finish school, not sleep with every willing woman.

"You could look at your room information on your phone." He pointed to the pink iPhone in her hand.

"Or you could take me back to *your* room." She leaned into him. "And help me figure out what bed I'm going to sleep in."

"I recommend using the app or checking your email." Grady turned, gritted his teeth, and walked back to his room. He closed the door and let out a sigh of relief that she hadn't followed him.

Grady leaned back on his bed, resting his head

against the wall. His mind went back to Room 1111. How he felt a strange pull both times as he walked by. Grady accessed the room database for his building and scrolled down the list until he came to the room in question.

Alida Zayvrus, bachelor's in psychology. It wasn't her academy record that caught his eye, but the light-gray eyes staring at him. She had long, curly blond hair. She'd left most of her information blank. No hobbies or favorite TV shows. The other person in the room was Rebecca Hart. She'd listed every vampire show. Her hobby was poetry.

Grady still didn't understand what caused him to almost stumble each time he walked by her room. It didn't matter how pretty Alida was—he had a mission, and she was not a part of it. Grady closed his laptop and rested his head against the wall.

His eyes had barely closed when someone knocked on his door again. Grady answered and found an older lady, more than likely someone's mother, waiting in the hall.

"Someone is having sex in the elevator," she whispered, and her face turned bright red. "Don't get me wrong, I'm not against sex, but it's a pain in the butt to carry the boxes up the stairwell. I didn't want to call the cops, but they won't stop."

"I'll take care of it." Sex in the elevator or hallway was one of the top complaints. Noise and alcohol were the top two.

Grady pressed the elevator's up button and waited for the elevator to stop on the second floor. The elevator dinged, and the door opened. Sure enough, a man had a woman pressed up against the elevator wall. Grady stuck out his foot, stopping the elevator door from closing.

"You guys need to find a room," Grady ground out.

The woman looked over the man's shoulder, but they didn't stop.

God, I hate this job. "The other option is I call the campus police, and you'll get kicked out before class even starts."

The girl at least had some brains. "Let me down." She pressed at the man's shoulders.

He stepped back, and she slid down the wall, straightening her dress. "Please don't call the cops."

"This is your first and *last* warning. No sex in the hallway, elevators, and the bathroom. Now go before I change my mind."

The guy finished buttoning up his pants and glared at Grady. "Watch yourself, RA. If you want to keep your job, you better stay out of my way. This is *your* first and last warning."

He was clearly another entitled student who thought his parents' money would let him break the rules. That never worked, no matter how many students tried. Typically, the student who made the threat didn't live in the dorm.

Grady ran a hand down his face and glanced down

at his Apple Watch. *Quarter past one.* The day was moving so slowly, and he still had three more move-in days left. As he turned to walk back to his room, a flash of pink ran by him—a streaker. Grady took off down the hall.

Streakers sucked. It wouldn't be easy to avoid touching the parts he preferred not to. Today's streaker was faster than he liked. Grady didn't spend his time in the gym running. He chose to lift weights.

When he neared Room 1111, the door was open, and Alida was standing outside. Next to her was a tall, muscular man, his arms crossed, with a scowl on his face. But Grady's eyes connected with Alida's.

His focus was no longer on the naked man running through the hall. Everything around him faded into the background. He blinked, and the spell was broken—the chase needed to end.

Grady leaped forward and took the streaker down to the ground. The guy screeched as he went down. Grady grabbed the guy by both arms and lifted him up.

"Where's your room?" Grady growled, and the guy nodded toward the way they first came.

Grady pushed the guy back down the hall but stopped. Alida blocked their way, her eyes trained on him. "Move."

Her pretty eyes narrowed. "That was rude."

"Or you can follow us. I wouldn't mind spending some time with you," the naked freshman said.

Her lip ticked up. "You shouldn't show off the

merchandise before asking a woman back. She already knows what you have, and...you should keep the clothes on."

"Hey, I'm average size."

The tall man next to Alida let out a sigh. "Alida, let the man do his job with the naked person. As for you, my daughter's right. You shouldn't be proud of being a streaker."

"I don't like you," the freshmen muttered as Grady pushed him forward. "But I wouldn't mind spending some time with her." The idiot turned to Alida's mother.

"Oh, honey, you have so much to learn in life. For one, you better work on your charm, because"—she waved her hand in front of the guy—"this will not get you far...unless you become good with your oral skills."

"Jesus, Mom," Alida muttered.

Her dad seemed to like the response, because he pulled the woman close and whispered something into her ear. And she smiled up at the tall, muscular man.

It was strange how young the couple looked, with a daughter who'd already finished a four-year degree. But he didn't have time to think about Alida and her family. He shoved the freshman forward.

He walked the kid down the hall to his room and waited for him to get dressed. The halls were clearing for the night, but later, he would have to deal with a new set of issues—probably noise complaints, because everyone wanted to party the Saturday before class started.

Grady went back to his room, closed the door, and rested his head against the pillow. Now would be the best time to get some rest before the parties started. His eyes closed, and in his dreams, he saw the gray-eyed angel from earlier. *Why the hell can't I get her out of my mind?*

She was even haunting him in his dreams. They were out in a field next to a stream, talking. The mountain breeze was cool. Grady had never left the DC area, so he had no clue why he would dream of the mountains. An enormous dragon flew over them, and a steam of smoke and fire escaped its mouth.

Grady threw his body over Alida to protect her, but the fire never came. But the scent of smoke increased. He searched the horizon. *No sign of fire...*

The smoke alarms in the building blared, and Grady jumped out of bed. He was losing his mind. Grady rushed out of his room to make sure the students got out safely.

3

ALIDA

*A*lida's first two nights in the dorms were entertaining. Saturday night, a student left his hot plate on, and a blanket caught fire. Luckily, the rude, sexy RA guy jumped into action. He had the fire out in seconds.

She grabbed her towel and clothes to take a shower in the community shower area. Even though Alida had grown up with lots of money, Kirin and Talia had always made sure she worked for everything she had. Still, the community showers were not something she was used to.

She glanced over at her roommate's bed. Talia hadn't seen her since the day she moved in, and the bed was still untouched. What really bothered her was the picture of Kael above the bed. Alida knew the photo bothered her father as much as it bugged her. He grumbled about the photo during lunch. She was just glad he hadn't demanded she move back home.

Uncle Kai had called her the night she moved in. A direct-to-TV movie about Kael had premiered a few weeks ago, and everyone was in love with it. Her family had worked for years cleaning up the mess the warlock had created, and she really didn't appreciate the daily reminder of him.

Alida took her time walking to the bathroom. She set her things on the counter then went into the shower and let the warm water trickle down her back. She would not let the low water pressure ruin her day. Nope. She was officially on her own and not counting on her parents to help her out.

When she finally could get the conditioner out of her hair, she grabbed her fluffy white towel and wrapped it around her body. She walked out of the shower to find none of her things were on the counter. She contemplated using her powers to get back into her room, but her mom's voice rang in her head. Both of her parents worried about her getting caught.

For years, Kael's men had come after her because she was one of the first experiments that had gone right. The embryo had been fertilized in a test tube before being transferred to the woman who would give birth to the baby. Despite his success with Alida, Kael had never been able to replicate her DNA or the process. That hadn't stopped other scientists from trying to get a glimpse of her DNA over the years.

She took a deep breath, tied the towel tighter around her body, and snuck out of the bathroom. When she reached her door, she jiggled the handle— and remembered that she'd locked it. *Fuck.*

A few students walked up and down the halls. A guy whistled at her, and she rolled her eyes. She glanced down the hall to the RA's dorm. God, she really didn't want to ask for his help. He seemed to have a permanent scowl on his face. When she was near him, she wanted to know more about him, but he didn't seem to have the same feelings.

Steeling her nerves, she walked down the hall and knocked on his door. She could hear him walking around in the room, but he didn't answer. With an aggravated sigh, she knocked on the door again.

Grady swung the door open, with his usual scowl on his face. But that wasn't the first thing she noticed. Nope. The man didn't have a shirt on. His hair was tousled, and a bunch of weights lay on the floor of his room.

"You're naked," Alida muttered.

"So are you, and you're in the hall," Grady said, not looking up from her chest.

Her cheeks felt like they were on fire.

Grady leaned forward, grabbed her elbow, and pulled her into his room. His eyes scanned her body again. "Why are you walking around the halls half-naked, Alida?"

Alida closed her eyes, trying to block out his scent.

He smelled so good, and it was amplified by being in his room.

"Wait. How do you know my name? And someone stole all of my things from the bathroom while I was in the shower," she snapped back.

"I know the name of everyone on my floor."

A flash of emotion crossed Grady's face so quickly that if she hadn't been watching closely, she would've missed it. *Anger? Annoyance?* She could easily go into his mind and figure out what he felt. She kept her powers locked up tightly, though.

Every second he kept his shirt off, Alida found it harder to stand still, especially while she was naked under her towel. She needed to remember one thing: he was a crabby RA who was nothing but rude. *Even if he has abs for miles. God, how does he even have that many abs?*

He didn't make a move toward the door to help her with the current issue.

"So, are you going to help me with my door?" She placed one hand on her hip, causing her towel to dip a little.

"Uhhh." Grady ran his hand over his face before grabbing a T-shirt and shorts from the bed. "Here, put these on. You're not walking back out there naked."

"I have a towel on. It's not like my bits are hanging out." She grabbed the clothes from his hand. When he didn't turn around immediately, she dropped the towel to the ground. *Now* her bits were showing.

Grady's eyes widened before he turned. "Was that necessary? You could've told me you were about to change."

Alida pressed his shirt to her nose before slipping it over her head. It smelled like him. She pulled up his shorts and analyzed Grady for a second. His back muscles flexed as he waited for her to tell him she was finished changing. Grady was one of the first people who'd made her confused. She'd never cared what someone thought about her. But she wanted Grady to like her. Instead, he seemed on edge around her.

"You can turn around." Instead of walking to the door, she sat down in his computer chair. "Can I ask you something?"

"Doesn't look like you're going to give me a choice," he replied.

"I'm persistent." Alida shrugged. "Is it still possible to change rooms after a couple days?"

"Yes, it is your roommate giving you problems?"

"You will think I'm strange."

"Really? Now you care what I think. I've seen you naked. We are clearly to the stage where you can tell me your problems."

She liked the joking side of Grady. His blue eyes sparkled when he smiled, and it made her feel like she could talk to him about anything—even if she wanted to move because her roommate had hung a poster on the wall. God, she was even embarrassed to ask the question. "She gives me a creepy vibe. Also, nobody enjoys sleeping next to a skull."

Grady narrowed his eyes. "You want to move because of a skull? I can tell you it won't pass as a reason."

She couldn't tell him about the picture. "I haven't seen her since the day I moved in. And she gave off bad vibes."

Grady shrugged. "People are strange, but wouldn't you rather have a roommate who's never here than one who might snore?"

"I'd prefer the one who doesn't make me feel like I have to sleep with one eye open," Alida murmured. "I need to get to class. Will you open my door or not?"

He nodded and opened the door. She followed him down the hall, watching his ass flex with each step. It surprised her when he stopped at her door and put the key in. Over the last couple of days, she'd seen him in the halls, but she had no clue he knew where her dorm was.

She'd dated a few times in high school, but most of her boyfriends were too scared to date her for very long. It wasn't easy hiding that your dad was the head of the West Virginia council when you went to a shifter school. Getting her undergrad hadn't been much different, because Dunes Community College was only a few miles from the town she'd grown up in, and most of the students were getting degrees so they could work at the council. Her parents had also talked her into living at home while she worked on her degree.

When she'd tried going to college parties, one of her dad's men seemed to always be watching her. But now she was on her own and hours away from any shifter school or town. Alida wouldn't have been surprised to find out that her dad had sent one of his enforcers to protect her in DC as well. She needed to keep an eye out. Most people wouldn't see the well-trained mercenaries, but Alida had grown up with them around. She knew the tricks and places they hid when watching someone.

Grady walked into her room, and the dorm seemed to shrink when filled with his presence. Her place was half the size of Grady's. The door closed behind him as he watched her for a second. "You'll need to fill out a report in regards to the stolen items. "

"Will it get me my things back?" She knew it wouldn't, and it would be a pain in the ass. Nothing was going like she'd hoped so far.

"No. But you're going to need a new key. Maybe even pay to have the locks changed on your dorm, but you're going to need to let your roommate know about the change, so she doesn't have an issue getting in."

Maybe the change wouldn't hurt. Locking her roommate out wasn't an awful idea. Making enemies in her first week wasn't the best idea, though. "I'll make sure to do that, and thanks for letting me in."

"Find me after class so I can open the door again. You will not want to leave the place unlocked."

"Sure, maybe my roommate will be back by then." That way, she wouldn't have to bother him.

Her heart raced as Grady stepped closer to the center of the room, but then he turned to stare at the poster on the wall. "At least she has good taste in movies."

The air in the room became thick. Alida's pulse beat a mile a minute. She'd never watched much regular TV. Her preferred choice was more likely a Netflix movie or spending time outside.

"You like fictional supernatural movies?" she asked.

Except it wasn't fictional, and now Alida wanted to watch the movie to really find out how close the film was to real life. It depended on who'd made the movie —one of Kael's followers or someone who worked for the council.

"I watch a lot of fantasy and supernatural movies. I am surprised to see this, though."

"Why?" She hoped she didn't sound too eager to figure out more of what was going on.

"The film was only released a few weeks ago, and it was straight to TV. The magical effects were amazing, but the storyline was far too unbelievable."

"So, supernatural storylines aren't believable?"

She was honestly curious about his answer. Few humans came to Haven Springs, and when they did, she didn't speak to them.

"I'm not saying someone turning into a wolf or dragon is believable. But that story had a girl who could transport and read minds. Now that was going a little far."

"So you had an issue with the little girl in the film?" she asked, trying to hold back some of her anger. "But the warlock changing people into shifters was okay?"

Fuck. She couldn't take the words back now. And she hoped the storyline matched the actual life for a second, or she would have to figure out a way to backtrack.

Grady raised his brow. "So you've seen it?"

Nope, she'd lived the nightmare. "Well, he looks like a warlock and a human holding a syringe in the background to a human and wolf. Hell, the name of the movie is *Transformation*. It wasn't that hard to figure out what the plot was from the poster."

"Okay, you just got it really close."

"You still didn't answer the question. You didn't have an issue with the warlock, but the little girl bothered you—she wasn't even good enough to show up on the poster."

"You really want to stand here and debate a movie you haven't seen? And a second ago, you wanted to move rooms because your roommate has that." He pointed to the skull on the table. "By the way, the skull on the nightstand is fake."

She ignored his jab about the skull, not wanting to tell him the poster was the real reason. "You still haven't answered the question." She knew she should drop the subject, but it really bothered her he had an issue with her. It wasn't like he knew he was insulting her powers. She should have been happy that a human would consider her powers unbelievable. Some days, she worried about what power she would get next, because they hadn't stopped forming.

"Fine. The girl kept getting more and more powers. Seemed like the writers went a little overboard...and they threw her dead parents into the mix by having her see their ghosts. I don't like it when movies try to put ghosts in with shifters. But the special effects were good. And the little girl's new dad and his brothers were badass."

She wanted to roll her eyes. Everyone thought her dad and uncles were badass. But it was Talia, Lucy, and Nyx who were the real heroes of the story. "Maybe I'll have to watch it this weekend."

Grady snorted. "You think you can handle a dark supernatural movie when you couldn't even handle a fake skull and some black sheets on the bed?"

Anger bubbled in Alida, and she flipped a hand toward the door. It flew open. Grady turned and stared at it for a second before turning back to her.

"I think it's time you go. I'll return your clothes later." She was going to ignore the fact that the door had flown open, and she hoped he did the same, because she had no clue what to say. She was too pissed.

"Sure." He stared at the door a second longer before walking out. When he stepped outside the threshold, he turned. Before he could say a word, she flipped her hand again, and the door shut. *Fuck.* She used her magic to lock the door and fell back onto the small twin bed.

Well, that didn't go as planned. After only three days, she'd already used her magic in front of a human.

4

GRADY

*T*he door had just closed on its own. Alida had been standing on the other side of the room when he walked out. Before he could ask if she wanted to watch the movie together, the door had slammed in his face. It wasn't like a cross breeze could close the door in the middle of the dorm building.

I have to be losing my mind. For one, he almost asked if she wanted to spend the night watching a movie with him. But Grady didn't have time for women. He needed to concentrate on school so he could get out and start making a living for himself.

He would not let the drug-addicted mother and the life he'd been born into shape his future. He'd worked hard to move out of the trailer park and go to school. His mind went back to the blonde in the dorm room. He figured her life was easy. She had loving parents and money, and she'd never had to worry where her next meal might come from. Her biggest worry was her strange roommate, who hadn't even shown up in two days.

He'd noticed the designer purse on the end table, along with the state-of-the-art laptop. The thing looked powerful enough to be used for gaming. He highly doubted either of the women in that dorm room had ever even played a game on the computer. Alida seemed like someone who would spend her time at the mall.

Grady opened his dorm room and quickly changed into a pair of black pants and a white button-down shirt. He glanced at the clock—he had half an hour before he had to go TA Organizational Behavior. He checked the roster and noticed Alida's name on the sheet. Grady stopped himself from walking back down the hall and asking to walk her to class.

He didn't have time for a romance or a high-main-tenance woman. Even if they were both working on their master's degrees. It wasn't often a graduate student moved into the main dorms.

Grady grabbed his things and rushed across campus to the classroom. Professor Miles was in the room already, going over the syllabus for the day. Grady liked the old professor. He taught from experience as well as the book. He didn't spend four hours going over PowerPoints. The class would be interactive.

"Hello, Grady," Professor Miles said, looking over his black reading glasses. "Ready for another year?"

"You have a full class this year. Word has gotten out you're the professor to take."

"Well, the class has more females than males. Maybe they are coming to ogle at my TA."

"I don't think that is the case." A fair share of his students had asked him out the year before.

In his first year at college, he enjoyed spending time with freshmen and going to parties. Now, graduation was his only focus. But he couldn't get the blonde out of his head. Alida was beautiful.

Maybe another session at the gym after class would help keep his mind off her beautiful breasts. He still couldn't believe she'd dropped her towel in front of him before grabbing his shirt and shorts. Controlling his dick had grown even more challenging as she scowled at him after the movie comments.

Grady gathered the syllabus and the worksheet for the day and set them out in two piles so the students could grab them before walking to their seats. His damn mind went back to Alida, wondering if she would sit in the front or in the back.

There were five stadium rows of seats in a half-circle. The room could fit fifty-five students, and that was how many had enrolled in the class. Most students showed up on the first day, then they would see a trickle off on class size as it got further into the semester.

Fifteen minutes before class started, students streamed into the room. The air shifted as Alida walked through the door, grabbed the syllabus and worksheet. She looked up, and her gray eyes widened when she saw him. He couldn't help but smirk. Grady liked the fact that he'd caught her off guard.

"Why are you in my class?" she growled under her breath as she picked the papers.

Grady shrugged. "I'm the TA for this class."

She nodded before turning. He couldn't help but watch her ass sway in the tight jeans. A workout would not help get her out of his mind. Maybe if he slept with her, everything would be better.

She turned and sat in the front row—directly in front of where he sat. When she leaned forward, he caught sight of her white lacy bra under her T-shirt. He couldn't stop himself from glancing again.

Professor Miles stood and went through the syllabus. Grady couldn't help but peer at Alida. She was focused on her phone, not paying attention to a word the professor said. For some reason, it agitated him. Half of the class spent their time on their phone, but when Alida did the same thing, he wanted to call her out for the blatant disrespect.

With an hour left of class, Professor Miles got a text that he needed to deal with, and he left Grady to finish teaching the course for the day. They were to the question-and-answer part of the assignment.

"Can anyone tell me what the author wanted you to

do after taking the study skills test?" The question was simple, and it was spelled out for them. The author wanted them to develop their own formula for academic success.

Nobody raised a hand. He usually had one or two, but not one in this class.

He turned his gaze to Alida. "Can you tell us?" Grady glanced at the sheet of names, pretending to pick one. "Alida?"

Her eyes shot up from her phone. He figured she wouldn't know the simple answer to developing her own formula for academic success.

"Of course. The author wanted us to develop a formula for academic success."

He frowned. She'd practically read his mind. "And what motivation can the student use to help create these goals?" Grady wanted to smirk, because he knew she hadn't read the information.

"Easy. Set learning goals, create interesting tasks, and have a positive attitude. Something you don't have," she mumbled under her breath, and a few of the people next to her chuckled.

He wanted to know how she was figuring out the answers. It seemed almost like she was reading someone's mind, because she hadn't even read the article. Her eyes went back to her phone, and he couldn't help but be irritated that she wasn't paying attention.

For the next hour, he picked on other students to

answer questions, while she didn't listen to a word he was saying. With only five minutes left of class, he dismissed everyone but asked Alida to stay.

"I'll get you your clothes back after my next class," she reminded him, and his mind went back to her naked in his dorm.

"It's not the clothes I want to talk to you about. Alida, it's your first day of class, and you couldn't take your eyes off your phone." While he waited for her answer, he shoved the excess paper into his backpack.

"Just because my eyes were on my phone didn't mean I wasn't paying attention."

"I'm still wondering how you answered the questions without reading the paper."

She shrugged. "If you think I wasn't paying attention, ask me another question," she said with a twitch of her lips.

This would be his chance to prove her wrong about listening. "Which type of behavior modifications relies on consequences?"

They hadn't discussed that topic in class. They would study operant conditioning later in the semester.

"Well, to start with, that wasn't something we went over today. But to answer the question, it's operant conditioning. Now, if you don't mind, I need to grab a bite to eat before my next class."

He shoved his arm through the backpack strap and

threw it over his back. Her slight smile made him feel frustrated and turned on at the same time. When she ran her tongue along her lips, his eyes flickered down.

"I never pictured you as a psychology buff," he murmured. He took a step toward the door. "I figured you rode on your parents' coattails."

"Rude," she said, pulling her textbook closer to her chest. "My parents made me work for everything I have. Learning was a big thing in our house. We already have enough scientists in my family. It's none of your business, but I wanted to help shift…humans with coping."

Grady chuckled. "Humans?"

Her lips moved to say something else, but she clamped them together for a second. "The other option is psychology for depressed animals."

"A pet therapist?" he asked, unable to hold back his laughter.

"Why not?"

"First, pets don't talk back. And who is going to pay for their animal to see a therapist?"

Alida arched her perfectly manicured brow. "I had two cats growing up, and when one died, the other seemed depressed. My mother called a pet therapist, and it helped."

"So you studied psychology so you can use it on animals later. Then why are you majoring in business," he asked, actually curious about her answer.

"Not sure how you know my undergrad is in psychology. When I first went to school, I wanted to become a psychologist. Now I want to help my dad, hence the MBA." Her lips ticked up at the end, like she knew something he didn't.

He heard her stomach growl. "How much time do you have between classes?"

Alida glanced down at a gold watch with a crystal face. "Almost an hour."

Grady offered her an empty smile. "How about I buy you lunch as a peace offering?"

"Sure, but I get to pick."

He nodded and followed her down the hall and out of the building. They were next to the student union, which had several places to choose from. To his surprise, she got in line at the burger restaurant. But he wasn't ready for how much she ordered. He figured it was a way to pay him back for being a prick. Instead of calling her out, he spent. There was no way she could eat more than a quarter of the food.

Once they sat down, he watched as she wrapped her ruby-red lips around the straw and took a sip of her milkshake. Grady had settled for water and one burger. He figured she would have enough left over if he was still hungry.

"So what made you want to be a TA and RA? Aren't those some of the worst jobs?" Alida asked before popping a fry into her mouth.

Grady tried not to stare at her lips. "I'm here on a grant and scholarship. The RA and TA pay for the rest of my college. I didn't have anyone to help me." He hadn't meant for the last part to come out.

"That's amazing. I'm happy I could go here."

"Why? Would you have gone somewhere else?"

"My parents...well, my dad didn't want me to go far from home. He's worried I'm going to get kidnapped again out in the world."

"Someone kidnapped you?"

Her eyes widened like she'd told a family secret. The more he got to know Alida, the more questions he had.

Alida took the last bite of her first burger and unwrapped her second before answering. "It wasn't anything very big. Forget I said that. My dad and mom just worry about me."

He grabbed his sandwich and took a bite. He was only a quarter of the way done with his sandwich, and she was already half finished with her second.

"So when you weren't getting kidnapped, what did you do for fun?"

Alida placed her sandwich on the table then wiped her face with a napkin. "My parents are really close to my uncles, and they have kids. I'm the oldest by a lot, so I spent a lot of time babysitting. We'd also spend a lot of time in Florida at my parents' friends'. They had a youth camp in Cassadaga, Florida."

For someone who feared her roommate over a skull

and poster, she should have been worried about the place where she'd gone in Florida. Cassadaga had the most rumors about its town. Anybody who researched or studied the supposed supernatural world knew about Cassadaga and the psychics. "You spent time in the psychic capital of the world but fear your roommate."

"It's…" The smile fell from her face, and she pushed her food away. "The reason doesn't matter. And I decided I'm going to deal with the roommate issue."

"I wasn't making fun of you."

He wished he could take back the words to see her smile again. Instead, she shook her head and glanced down at her watch.

When she said nothing, he muttered, "I had a terrible childhood, so I watched any supernatural or fantasy show I could get my hands on." He'd never told anyone about his past.

She eyed him for a second. "My uncle Kai and his scientist wife are huge supernatural movie buffs. He's also a big game nerd."

Grady tapped his finger on the table. "Are you into games?"

Her nose scrunched up, and she shook her head. "Nope, totally not computer literate. I take notes and do everything by hand. As far as research, I love the library and spend time reading."

Alida hadn't asked any more questions about his childhood, and it made him feel less exposed.

41

Her phone buzzed, and she frowned at it. "I'm sorry. It's my dad, and I need to take this."

He nodded, and she stood and walked away. Whatever her father said made tears run from her eyes. It took everything not to run to her side that second. And he wanted to kill the person who'd made her sad.

5

ALIDA

$\mathcal{O}$ne phone call from her dad, and her perfectly thought-out future could be in jeopardy. Five days ago, her dad had called to tell her that her roommate had been murdered. Well, not exactly murdered. Nope, she'd belonged to a cult, and all its members had committed suicide as a sacrifice to Kael.

The police had closed the case as a hazing gone wrong, but her dad and uncles didn't believe it. Her uncle Kai had hacked the local police department and read the report. Kirin had sent a team to do their own investigation. Fifteen college students recruited to join the sorority had died around a shrine. Kai had taken the shrine photos off one of the sorority girl's Facebook pages. On the shrine was a picture of Kael.

Talia had promised her that no ritual could ever bring Kael back to life. But from the shakiness in her mother's voice, Alida suspected she was hiding something. Alida thought about transporting home, where she could read her mother's mind. She didn't want to go back to her dorm room and see all the reminders of her roommate. That was why she'd slept on the couch in the common room every night since her father told her the news. It had taken two days before the school notified her about what had happened to Raven.

Not only was she worried about sleeping in her room alone, but she also didn't want to deal with the poster on the wall as a reminder of how the girl had lost her life. She knew she could probably take it down, but touching someone else's things felt strange. Alida hoped the school or Raven's parents would come soon to collect the items.

The sexy RA would have the answers, but she wasn't ready to talk to him yet. In a very creepy way, she kept wearing his athletic shorts and T-shirt to bed each night. It really needed to be washed, but his scent calmed her. She knew she would have to face him soon.

Over the past week, she would feel his presence at the entrance of the common area. He never came in, only watched her from the doorway before heading to his room. Some nights, she would wake up with a blanket covering her.

The past few nights, people had come in to watch a movie on TV or to study at the table to the side. Tonight she was the only one sitting around watching TV on the second full weekend. She heard other students talking about all the parties, a few talked about heading home. A quick trip home had crossed her mind a few times during the week, but she didn't want to use her parents as a crutch. It was time for her to stand on her own and not rely on them to keep everything bad away from her.

Her dad had made her promise not to ditch the bodyguard he'd sent. The negotiations with her dad had taken thirty minutes. He wanted a guard by her side every second of the day, but how would she explain having a bodyguard when she was in class or her dorm room? They'd compromised by agreeing to one bodyguard outside the buildings and her checking in periodically. She'd had the same guard for years, so she also knew he would report every little thing back to her dad.

In her mind, her bodyguard was her excuse for not going to parties. Shifters couldn't get drunk anyway, unless they drank Arrow's special brew, which had secret magical elements that caused shifters to feel the effects of alcohol. Her mom could get a buzz, but it took a lot of wine. Alida had tried alcohol over the years, and she'd never cared for the taste. She also worried about not being able to control her powers if she drank too much.

As if on cue, the promo for *Transformation* flashed across the screen. It showed a small girl with blond locks. Alida was impressed by how closely the character resembled her. Maybe it was time she watched the movie to see how much they got right and wrong.

There was no way they would have all aspects of what happened. Alida curled up and pulled the blanket closer.

She'd been eight when Kael had her parents killed. She still remembered standing over her parents' lifeless bodies. Then everything happened so fast, mercenaries from the council showed up and cuffed her before taking her to the council headquarters in West Virginia. That was where she'd met Talia, the only person who'd stood up for her in the beginning. Talia had saved Alida's life then became her new mom.

At times, though, she wished she could still see the ghost of her other mom. Not because of anything Talia or Kirin did, but just because she missed her. Technically, Maya hadn't been her mom, either. Jalil had genetically engineered Alida in a test tube. Her dad, Jalil, had taken the research and destroyed it. When she was a baby, her powers were more potent than anything they had seen, and he'd worried that the information would get into the wrong hands.

When Kael found out about Alida, he wanted to use her DNA to create his own super soldiers. The military would pay any number to Kael. But when Jalil refused to give up the information, Kael had him killed, along with her mom. At the time, Kael used Gideon's magic to cover up his wrongdoings. He'd gone so far as to frame Alida for the murder, but it was Talia and Kirin who'd proved she was innocent.

That hadn't stopped Kael from starting his own

research anyway. He'd opened labs all over the country, recruiting and kidnapping the best scientists who specialized in DNA. Some didn't even know their research was being used to turn humans into shifters.

A movement to the side caught her attention, and Grady walked into the room, holding a bowl of popcorn and a bag of candy. "Mind if I join movie night?"

She pulled her legs in so he could sit at the other end. Instead, he stopped where her head was and motioned for her to sit up. He sat, put the popcorn on his lap, and wrapped an arm around her. She couldn't help but melt into his side. A wave of embarrassment rushed over her as she realized she was still wearing his clothes.

Some worry about her life washed away, though. Nobody ever had that kind of effect on her. It was almost like he was her mate...She hadn't even thought about that. It had taken Kirin over three hundred years to find Talia. Alida never expected to find her mate at a young age. All the signs were making sense now, though. She couldn't stop thinking about him. Whenever he was near, all the worry went away. His smell alone calmed her at night. His shirt didn't smell much like him anymore and more like her lavender soap.

"I'm going to watch this *Transformation* movie you talked about. See if it's really as good as you think," she joked.

He grabbed his chest in mock horror. "Then you

can see for yourself how the girl character was so unbelievable."

A wave of sadness washed over her. What if he was her mate, and he didn't like her or ran for the hills when she had to tell him everything about her life? Could she live without him?

She closed her eyes and turned her attention back to the TV. The opening scene was Talia and Kael arguing before she came into the interrogation room. A chill ran down her arms, remembering how cold they'd kept the place. She could see her breath as she sat, waiting for someone to talk to her. They had said nothing from the time they dragged her out of her house until they stuck her in that room—where there was a knife on the table. For a long time, she'd attempted to use her powers to move it, but she couldn't in the interrogation room. It was like she was human.

"I was joking about the little girl," he murmured, jerking his head toward the TV.

She shook her head, trying to get out of the past. It was hard while she was watching a reenactment of the worst and best year of her life. She already knew what would happen next—the vision in Talia's mind. She'd never asked to see the murder or understand what had happened. Alida's eyes widened as she watched the supposed make-believe murder of her parents. She didn't know how much was true.

"Alida, are you sure you want to watch this?" Grady

asked, brushing the tear from her cheek. "You know this is all made up, right? Never mind, let's watch something else."

Grady grabbed the remote and changed the channel right when it got to the part where Alida had transported Talia and herself out of the room and back to her childhood home. Not even thinking, Alida used her powers to turn the TV back to the movie.

"What the fuck?" Grady grumbled, pressing the channel button again.

Alida clicked it back with her mind. "Leave it, please. I want to watch this."

He eyed her for a second before placing the remote on the table. She was glad when he didn't try to figure out why the TV kept changing back to the movie. She knew it was stupid to use her powers, but something had come over her. And if he really was her mate, he would figure it out at some point, and hopefully, not run from her.

"See the transport part? That was a little unbelievable."

"Why?" she asked, her eyes not leaving the screen.

"She can transport them back to the house but not know if someone was in it. Also, real-time travel? That was a little overkill." Grady popped a piece of popcorn into his mouth.

Alida had moved through time once in her life, and she'd never tried again. She worried she would mess the timeline up or, worse, get stuck in a time she didn't want to be in. "You realize everything in the movie is part of the plot? It adds to the story. Wondering if they will accidentally time travel instead of transporting to the next location."

"I guess," he muttered as he ran his fingers up and down her spine. "Now comes the good part. The hero is about to show up."

Alida wanted to roll her eyes at Grady for calling her dad a hero. He would always be that to her. Back then, she'd seen two futures, one where he turned them in and another where he helped them. "I bet the little girl is the hero in the story," she said, grabbing the box of candy out of Grady's hand.

"You know…that actor and even the actress look a lot like your mom and dad. She's even wearing gloves like your mother had on."

"I see the similarities. Mom wears gloves because her circulation is bad and she has icy hands." Growing up, Alida had never had to explain the gloves to anyone. Everyone knew why Talia wore them, and if she didn't have them on, they wouldn't come close. Not everyone liked the idea of someone seeing their past mistakes. Poor circulation was a pretty weak excuse, but it was all she could think of on the fly. Grady didn't question it. He just continued to watch the movie.

Neither of them spoke much during the rest of the movie. Alida was worried by how accurate the movie was. The only thing they didn't have to a T was the inside of Kai's lair. Everything else, including the cabin, was eerily similar to the real thing. Now she knew why her parents were worried.

"So do you agree, parts were a little over-the-top?" Grady said.

Alida snorted. "Nope. Still think the girl was the hero. Also, think Kael deserved a far worse death."

"Really?" Grady's eyes narrowed. "I never pictured you for someone who would think death was the answer without a fair trial."

"Of course. Anyone who kills that many people deserves the same. And that was only the people the movie showed. There are probably others." There were. Many people had died because of the asshole. "As for a trial? They called the shifter king. Who else would you want at the trial? He's dangerous and has minions. Hell, he's fake, and some people still think he's alive. A fictional character just caused a bunch of people to die. For what?"

Grady cocked his head to the side. "You're right. I never looked at it like that. Also, I'm sorry about your roommate. Is that why you've slept out here for the past week?"

She nodded.

He pulled her into his arms. "You want to stay with me tonight?"

For a second, she couldn't believe he'd asked her. And she wanted it more than anything. So she nodded and followed him down the hall.

6

GRADY

*G*rady stretched on his small couch. Sleeping on the couch was horrible, but he'd known he wouldn't be able to keep his hands off Alida's gorgeous body if he joined her in his bed. He looked over at the bed—she was gone.

He still couldn't believe he'd asked her to stay in his room for the night. The words had just slipped out of his mouth. It was almost like how he couldn't stop himself from joining her in the common area. Each night, it killed him to see her alone. Then he'd gotten the report on what had happened to the roommate.

They'd said she was pledging a sorority and it was a hazing gone terribly wrong. He wasn't suspicious by nature, but that sounded strange. So he'd spent the last few nights watching over her in the common area. Something was off. Or he was finally losing his mind.

His phone vibrated across the room. Worried it might be a professor, he threw the covers off and got up. Stretching, he walked across the small dorm room. An unknown number flashed across the phone screen. Grady hit the decline button and placed his phone back on the desk. It was way too early to deal with telemarketers. He had all of his professor numbers on his phone.

The smell of Alida filled his room, and his mind went back to her in his clothes. He didn't mind that she'd kept his shorts and shirt. Hell, if he was honest, he loved seeing her wear his clothes.

When his phone vibrated again, the same unknown number appeared. He grabbed his running shoes and went outside. A long run would help get his mind off Alida and back on track. She was a distraction, which was not something he needed so close to the end. He would finish school soon and look for a job. Grady would change his future.

Saturday was the one day he gave to himself. Sundays, he reserved for schoolwork. Mount Vernon loop was about five miles. His feet beat against the trail as he crossed over a small bridge. The path was empty. It was early, and he wondered where Alida had gone. *Back to her room?*

He cleared his mind and went back to running, enjoying the fresh air. Hearing footsteps behind him, he moved over to the side. A hand wrapped around his mouth before he had time to fight, then he felt a sharp prick to his neck. And the world slowly faded way as his body hit the grass.

GRADY'S HEAD HURT. The fog started to clear, and his memory came back. He was out on the run to clear his mind when someone put a needle in his neck. *Fuck.*

Before he opened his eyes, he moved his wrists and feet and let out a sigh. He wasn't tied down. He wasn't sure he would have known what to do if he was.

This was his first time being kidnapped, and whoever had taken him was going to be sad. Nobody would pay a ransom. He was sure nobody would care if he disappeared. Then his mind went to Alida. Would she notice he hadn't shown up to class on Monday? Or maybe one of his professors would call someone.

He opened his eyes. The room was large and fancy. If he had to make a guess, he was in a high-end hotel suite. At least his captors had the decency not to shove him on a dirty mattress in a basement. He rolled over on the bed and saw a bottle of water. Staring at the bottle, he wondered if it was safe to drink, but why would someone drag him into a hotel to kill him? That would have been easier back on the trail.

Grady grabbed the bottle, twisted off the top, and drank the warm liquid. It didn't do much to help the dryness in his mouth. There wasn't time to sit around and wait to see what happened next. He walked across the large room, admiring the crystal chandelier hanging from the ceiling. Grady grabbed the door handle and turned it, but it didn't budge.

They'd locked it from the other side. He looked around the room. Maybe the window would be his key out. But when he went to the window, his frustration mounted. He was high in a hotel in downtown DC. At least they hadn't taken him far.

The doorknob to the room twisted a couple seconds before the door opened. He reached for the lamp on the table, but it didn't move. Grady was about to come face-to-face with the person who'd kidnapped him.

When the door swung open, he was speechless and angry. His mother, the only person he hated more in the world, stood in the doorway, dressed in a red designer dress. Her brown hair was perfectly straight. She held a designer purse and wore matching heels, making her almost his height. No matter how much makeup she wore or the lovely clothes she had on, it wouldn't change the person she was. Case in point, she had kidnapped him instead of calling. He wouldn't have answered if she'd tried to call, anyway.

"Grady," she said, annoyed. "Like always, you needed to make things difficult."

"I have no clue what you are talking about. And I'm leaving."

"You're not going anywhere. If you would've answered your phone, everything would've been so much simpler. Instead, you had to ignore my calls and make my men go pick you up."

"Didn't know it was you calling since I never gave you my number. Even if I knew it was you, I wouldn't have answered, so you've wasted everyone's time."

"You were always so dramatic. I'm surprised you're going into psychology instead of drama. Always thought someone was out to get you. 'Poor me.' You're a grown-ass man. Now it's time you pay me back for all the hassle you put me through."

Grady couldn't help but laugh. "Put you through?"

His mother nodded and tapped her heel against the floor. "It was your fault child services did a surprise check and found those drugs in the house."

He shook his head. "It had nothing to do with the fact that my clothes hadn't been washed in weeks or that I didn't have food to eat at school?"

Genuine hatred glowed in her eyes. "They promised me money if I had you. Then they tried to pay me less, and I spent years in jail. But everything changed. They are willing to give me the money now."

"And I care about you getting money, why? My life changed for the better the day the cops hauled you off to jail. So whatever plan you came up with, I want no part of it. And if you push me, I will put you back in jail."

"You don't have a choice." She took a step into the room, her heels clicking against the expensive marble.

"Really?"

There was nothing he would do to help her. He scrubbed a hand over his face and let out a sigh. "Tell me what you want so I can say no and be on my way. Because if I'm not back to my dorm soon, someone will come looking for me."

Her evil laugh filled the room. "Nobody will come looking for you if I don't want them to. Things have changed over the years. I have power and the ability to give you what you want and take everything away from you with one phone call."

He frowned. "What is it you think I want?"

"Easy. You want a decent job and money to be like every other person out there. If I didn't give birth to you, I would've never thought you were my son. After everything I've learned recently, I think you had more of your father in you than I thought. But since you have gone all furry, maybe, I'm wrong."

"Fifteen years, and you still haven't changed." With a sad smile, he shook his head and took a step toward the door. "Do what you want to me, but I will never help you."

He stepped around her and, noticing the central area was empty, let out a sigh. She didn't have any guards around. When he stepped into the living area, she followed him. Grady was halfway across the room when a hand gripped his biceps hard—way harder than he'd expected his mom's grip to be. He remembered her hard touch as a kid—the connection of her fist against his face. But he'd been eight, not twenty-four.

Grady ripped his arm out of her hand, and her red nails dragged across his skin, drawing blood. Fifteen years later, she hadn't changed. He hadn't expected her to. He also didn't want to be anywhere near her.

Her eyes fell to the mark on his arm. Her nostrils flared, and she crossed her arms. He saw not one flicker of remorse in her face. Grady had never hit a woman, and he wouldn't start now, no matter how much he hated the woman who stood in front of him. He turned to leave again.

"One million dollars," she murmured.

His feet stumbled for a second. That would be enough money for him to get his doctorate and open his own practice. Those were his dreams, but he knew he would have to spend years saving before he could even think about that option.

"One million dollars," she drawled again. All she needed was the evil laugh at the end.

But his feet still hadn't moved. He hadn't told her off, because the money would change his life. Would it be worth it?

"What do I need to do?" He hated himself for asking the question. Grady turned and followed his mother over to the sitting area. She sat down on the white couch, and he paced on the far side.

"Next time I call, I need you to answer. And then, you will need to go to a lab and have your blood tested. Your father doesn't believe you are his. Once we have the proof, I will give you one million dollars."

It sounded way too easy for the money. "I'm going to have to pass. Bye."

He turned to leave, to finally leave the woman who'd given birth to him and never see her again. The day the police had carried him out of the house, they'd handcuffed his mom. He'd thought that would be the last day he ever saw her. It wasn't like he covered his tracks, though, and he'd known she would get out of jail one day. But he'd never thought she would come looking for him.

"Tough," she murmured. "The person who needs your blood isn't going to back down. They've had people on you for weeks. How would you feel if something happened to that girl you were with last night?"

A chill ran down his spine. "Alida has nothing to do with this. Furthermore, everything you said today, you could have stopped me in person to tell me."

"I wanted to prove how easy it was for me to find you. The next time I call, you better answer, because if I have to send my men again, you will not like the outcome."

His body went rigid. "Why don't I just go get my blood drawn, and this guy can look at it?"

"He wants to do it in his lab. And the lab is under…construction."

"Fine." Just because he'd agreed did not mean he was going to follow through. He would figure out who was watching him and send them in another direction.

Alida meant too much to him. He would need to cut all contact with her.

Grady walked out of the hotel room and pressed the elevator button. When he stepped in, two large men dressed in jeans and black leather jackets stepped off, both wearing sunglasses. When the elevator door closed, Grady let out his breath and pressed the down button.

He didn't have his wallet or phone, so he ran back to campus. Luckily, the men hadn't taken him very far. His head pounded with each step he took. The sun was setting, making him run faster. He didn't want to be outside in the dark after already getting kidnapped once that day. The dorm was quiet as he walked down the hall and stopped outside Alida's dorm. But he didn't knock. He had to leave her alone.

When he went to his room and opened the door, a white piece of paper was on the floor. He picked it up, expecting it to be a note from Alida, but it was a picture of the two of them on the couch watching TV together. "I'm watching you" was scribbled across the top of the paper.

7

ALIDA

"*Y*ou're home!" Talia yelled before wrapping her in a welcoming hug.

Alida stayed in her mom's arms a couple seconds longer than usual. It was only a week since she moved away, and she missed her family. When she left Grady's room early in the morning, she had too many questions and didn't want to ask them over the phone. She slipped out of his room and into hers, then she'd changed out of his clothes and teleported home. Her dad would give her a lecture, but it was worth getting to see her mom, brother, and sister.

"Hey, Mom." She smiled before slipping away from the warm hug. Alida pulled out the barstool and sat at the kitchen counter while her mom took two coffee cups out of the cupboard. It was still early; the sun was only up a little. Her dad would already be at the council offices. Alida had purposely timed her teleport home for after he'd left.

"What happened?" Talia handed her a cup of coffee, her eyes searching Alida's face. She was worried.

Quietly, Alida asked, "How did you know Dad was your mate?"

Talia's eyes widened for a second before a smile spread across her face. "You were there for it, honey, but when I touched him, it was different. His entire life poured onto me in seconds. Some of it scared me at the time. But I also had to keep you safe, so I couldn't concentrate on the fact."

"Would you have walked away if he'd wanted to turn me over to the council?" Alida asked, remembering how mad Talia was once when Kirin wanted to follow Gideon's orders. At the time, he hadn't known Gideon was under a spell and giving wrong orders. "I saw three different futures back then."

This was the first time she'd told her mom she could see other paths. It was something she held close because it was scary what could happen. And she worried if she told anyone the different ways, they would try to make sure to go down the correct one. Deep down, she had a feeling she had to keep them to herself.

Alida wished she could see her own future, but anything that led to her future was grayed.

"You hold too much on your shoulders." Talia sighed. "At the time, I knew you were the most-important thing. No way would I have let Kirin take you in to the council. The need to be around Kirin was strong. But it's a lot more different for your dad than for me. His inner beast also demands he be close to me. Now tell me why you think you found your mate?"

"Whenever he's near, it's calm. Like I don't have to fight to keep my powers at bay." Alida always had to keep a shield around her mind to keep from reading everyone's minds.

"That is one of the big indicators of mates. They help you stay grounded, take away the bad in the world. Your father is the only one I can touch, and my powers do nothing. I'm at peace when I'm around him, and this young man is making you feel the same?"

"Yes."

"So why are you here, having coffee with me before the sun comes up and not with this young man?"

"He's human."

The words hung in the air. Talia didn't answer her immediately, and Alida was tempted to pry into her mom's thoughts.

"Does that bother you?" Talia finally asked.

"Not at all. I love Lucy, and she's human, but she also embraced the world more than some shifters do," Alida answered. "Grady isn't a scientist who studies DNA. He's working on his master's in psychology—the study of the brain. And furthermore, how do I explain everything? He'll probably try to have me committed to the psych ward. Also, he thinks the girl in the *Transfor-*

mation movie is unbelievable. His exact words were she was way over-the-top."

Talia smiled. "Does that bother you? He thought you were a little over-the-top. You need to stop and take a step back. From the sounds of it, you watched the movie. I'll admit your dad and I watched it this week. We're worried about how much of the movie is exactly true. Things people shouldn't know. Your dad is working to figure out that part. As far as being an outsider and not knowing about the supernatural world, I could see where he is coming from." Talia was always Alida's voice of reason, but that didn't mean she liked the answer.

It would be impossible for her to hide her abilities forever from him, especially since they would both end up living forever once bonded. "Still stung when he made a comment."

Laughter and giggles sounded seconds before Kara and Kyle stormed into the kitchen. With wide eyes, they ran to Alida and wrapped her in hugs.

Hearing a rumbling from the garage, Alida glanced up at her mom. She'd heard the sound a million times over the years. It was her dad's Harley pulling into the garage. But he was supposed to be at work.

Alida stood from the stool and made her way to the garage, where her dad was taking off his helmet. He set it to the side, popping the bike's kickstand with the heel of his work boots. He wore his black dress pants and a gray shirt. His low-riding motorcycle shut off with a flip of his thumb. When he looked in her direction, his eyes were bright yellow. His dragon was close to the surface. That would scare most people—and shifters—but she knew he would never hurt her. It was most likely because he was worried.

He took a few steps across the garage and wrapped his arms around her, pulling her into a deep hug. God, she missed home, but she wasn't going to tell her overprotective dad that. He would insist that she stay.

"Is everything okay?" Kirin asked with concern in his voice.

"Yes, I wanted to come home and visit with Mom." It wasn't an outright lie and held enough truth that he couldn't sense her untold words in the air. "Is there a reason you came back home?" she asked.

Her bodyguard would've called her dad the second he figured out she was gone. She still didn't know how he would've known, but she would not worry about that at the moment.

"It worried me when Boris called..." Kirin's arms tightened around her.

When they walked back into the house, Talia had pulled everything out for breakfast. She sent Alida a questioning look, and Alida shook her head. There was no way she was ready to tell her dad that she might have found her mate. The second he found out, he would send Uncle Kai on a computer search to pull up everything he could about Grady. And Alida wanted to find out more about him on her own.

As the family settled around the large table, Alida asked, "How was the trip to Florida?"

Candace probably wasn't happy with the news that she was having twins, but the woman was the best mother.

"It was amazing. The camp is closed to the public, so we spent some time out by the lake."

Alida had spent much of her summer swimming in the lake in Florida. It was one of the vacation spots where they didn't have to worry about anyone knowing they were shifters. It was also where she lost her virginity to her long-time friend, Carl, who was a wolf shifter. They were close to the same age and had grown up together. They'd dated for years, both knowing they would find their mates one day. Carl had always been more confident than she was. A wolf wanted nothing more than to see the other person who completed them. Alida hadn't understood that feeling until she met Grady.

Alida stared at her dad for a second. "Did you tell Hunter about the babies?"

"No!" He laughed. His eyes swung over to Talia. "There wasn't much time."

She rolled her eyes. "Are you saying the big, bad dragon was scared to tell someone their future?"

"Hell, yes!" he grumbled. "She was running after eight kids already. That poor woman is going to kill Hunter when she figures out what is happening."

Kara cleared her throat next to Alida. "I'm going to

marry Joe when I grow up." Her younger sister had the biggest smile on her face. "And we are going to have as many kids as Aunt Candace and Uncle Hunter."

"Not happening," Kirin ground out. "My girls will stay single for the rest of their lives. No man is good enough for either of you."

Talia glanced across the table and folded her arms. "But Kyle can find his mate?" Her voice dropped low and deadly.

"It's not the same," Kirin shot back, wincing.

"Wrong. Both of my girls can end up with anyone they want." Alida's mother winked in her direction.

"That's good, because I already kissed Joey," Kara proclaimed to everyone.

The air in the room grew thick until Talia rested her hand on Kirin's arm. "Only time will tell."

Alida couldn't control when she had her visions. Certain events would trigger them, and the world around her would stop. Everything faded away, and a movie would play out—a movie sometimes she didn't want to see but was forced to.

She saw her little sister all grown up, standing at the altar with Joey. The little girl had found her mate. The person next to Alida was grayed out, and she couldn't see the people in her future, just a glimpse of her sister being happy. Then the vision faded as fast as it had come.

"You'll get your happy ending," Alida said to her younger sister. She would not tell her it was with Joey, though. Alida didn't want to take the chance of messing up the future.

Kirin growled, and Alida couldn't help but smile. It was nice to be home, but she needed to get back to campus. After breakfast, she helped clean up before kissing her mom goodbye. Seconds later, she was again in her dorm room, staring at the poster on the wall.

Making the decision on her own, she climbed up, took down the poster, and laid it face-down on the bed. She fired up her laptop and got to work on her schoolwork for the following week. When she looked up and noticed the sun had set, she walked down the hall to Grady's room. She didn't want him to be mad at her for leaving, but she had so many emotions running through her mind.

The heavy door swung open. Grady's hair was standing up from running his hands through it. He frowned at her. "What do you want, Alida?"

This wasn't the same Grady she'd talked to only hours ago. Something had happened.

She straightened her back. "I came to thank you for letting me sleep in your room."

"Okay," Grady said. "If that's all, I need to get back to my schoolwork."

Alida narrowed her eyes. "Why are you so cold and rude?"

"I don't have time for this."

She hated that he was mean, so she opened her mind and listened. A woman's name crossed it, and that was all he had time to worry about. She quickly shut the connection down and blinked a couple times.

"Fine!" she said before turning on her heels and walking back to her dorm.

Grady called out her name, but she didn't stop. Nothing mattered. He was thinking of another woman. Alida climbed into bed and curled into a ball. She would give herself one night to cry over losing her mate because he didn't feel the same way about her as she felt about him.

8

GRADY

*I*t was the last class before Thanksgiving. Alida hadn't glanced at Grady once during the lecture. He should have gotten used to it. Since the day he told her to leave him alone, she hadn't said a word to him. He wanted to scream and tell her he was doing it for her own good. Instead, he'd kept his mouth shut for three months and watched her from afar.

She'd spent most of her time in the dorm, studying. To his relief, he hadn't seen her with another man, because he wasn't sure how he would handle that. Just the thought sent jealousy raging through his body.

Professor Miles finished going over the topics the final would cover. After the final, everyone would head home for the winter break. In the past, he'd loved those few weeks in December, when the dorm was empty and he didn't see anyone. Now he hated the fact he would not see Alida for a few weeks.

Alida walked up to the professor after he dismissed the class. Grady stood to the side, wondering what she was asking him about.

The professor motioned toward Grady before grabbing his things and leaving the classroom. She stared at him for a heartbeat before shaking her head.

He reached out and grabbed her elbow, stopping her from leaving. An electrical pulse vibrated through them, and he couldn't help but let go. His eyes widened as he stared at her arm.

"Sorry, didn't mean to shock you," Grady said as he swung his backpack over his shoulder. "Did you have a question about something?" His eyes darted to her lips as she ran her tongue over them. God, he missed her, and they barely knew each other.

"I'm having a hard time figuring out a couple of theories." She motioned to her textbook. "I asked if the professor had any ideas on what I could study so I could grasp it better."

He should have directed her to a website that could help her. Instead, he blurted, "Are you going home for Thanksgiving?"

"I'm not sure. I really need to figure this out. My brother and sister don't make it easy to study when they're around."

Grady took that tidbit of information and stored it away. He didn't know much about her family, except that her dad looked angry and overprotective. That was the last time he'd seen them come to visit her. He also hadn't seen her leave over the weekends, either.

"If you want, I can help you study over the long weekend," Grady said.

"Really?" she asked, surprised. But then she closed her eyes for a second. "Wait! Are you sure you don't have someone you want to spend the holidays with?"

"I don't have any family," he lied.

Her eyes narrowed for a second, but she said nothing. It was like she was reading his mind, which was utterly impossible to figure out. Most likely, he'd flinched when he said he didn't have a family. Rebecca was only the person who'd given birth to him. She'd never really been his mother. A mother wouldn't have treated a child the way she had.

"Are you sure? The last time we talked, you seemed to not want anything to do with me."

He winced, thinking about the tears he'd seen in her eyes when he'd told her to leave. He felt awful, but he was trying to protect her from his mother and whatever mess she'd gotten them into. He hadn't heard a word from her since they'd talked in the hotel. "I was an ass."

"That's an understatement," she huffed.

Grady grimaced at her words. "I deserve that. How about we make Thanksgiving dinner at the dorm and spend the weekend studying? I have to prepare for my finals as well. So maybe you could help me study by quizzing me." He was digging himself in deeper and couldn't stop. Letting the fear of his mom overrun him again wasn't something he wanted to do.

More than anything, he wanted to spend time with Alida. A memory of his mother telling him "You can't have everything in life" flashed through his mind before fading away.

"Sounds like a date." Her cheeks blushed a beautiful pink. "Sorry, a study date."

"I liked what you said earlier." He reached up and tugged one of her blond locks. "How about I walk you back to the dorm?" He grabbed her bag also and threw it over his other shoulder. The thing weighed a ton. He wondered how she'd held the bag with two fingers when it felt like she'd filled it with gold bricks.

Shaking his head, he opened the door, and she walked through. The day before Thanksgiving, the campus was like a ghost town. Movement across the quad caught his attention. A tall man dressed in black leather watched them as they walked. His gaze sent a chill down Grady's back. He picked up his speed and dashed into a nearby building, pulling Alida through the door. He turned and gazed back outside, and the man hadn't moved his eyes from the building they'd dipped into.

Fuck. They're coming for me again. He didn't know what to expect. His first idea—going to the police—crossed his mind again, but he had nothing to go on. Also, it wasn't illegal for his mother to ask him to see a doctor.

Alida's brow furrowed as she peeked around the corner, and her shoulder brushed against him. The smell of her lavender shampoo went straight to his groin. He hadn't washed his bedsheets for months because he loved the smell of her, but it was long gone now.

"Who are we running from? Ex-girlfriend?" she asked.

"No, there was a man watching us."

"Ohh." Her eyes darted back outside. "He's harmless. More of a tattletale than anything. Also, if you throw things at him, he growls."

Grady was trying to keep up with her train of thought. The man wasn't watching him. Nope. He was watching Alida—and she knew about it. *Why does she have a bodyguard? Is she in danger?* "Who is that?"

"My babysitter." Alida pulled him through the hall instead of walking back into the common area. "Let's make him work for the money he gets."

She grumbled as they cut through buildings, trying to lose her bodyguard. Grady didn't think that was the best idea, but whenever he was around her, his rational decision-making went out the window.

She turned and smiled at him mischievously as they cut through the last building and walked into the service entrance of the dorm building. He'd lived in the same dorm building for four years and had never used the back entrance. Alida, on the other hand, weaved through the doors like she'd done it a million times.

Alida wasn't taking her safety into concern. If she had a bodyguard, it was for a good reason. Instead, they were running from him. She dragged him up the back stairs and exited next to his room. He opened the door and pulled her in with him.

Grady could barely think with her so close, but he needed to know why she was running from the man outside. Grady would do anything to help protect her —as much as he could. He'd spent hours working out, but that didn't mean he was coordinated enough to fight.

Her phone dinged, and she pulled it out and smiled. "Hello, Mom."

He couldn't hear the other side of the conversation, but Alida rolled her eyes and plopped down on the couch. After a minute, she said, "Boris has been overeating. I figured he needed a good chance to keep his skills up." He heard laughter on the other side before Alida spoke again. "I promise not to run anymore, but I got to go, Mom. Love you." Alida swiped her finger across the screen before she turned her attention back to Grady. "So, the big growly guy is Boris."

"Why do you have a bodyguard, Alida?"

"My dad's a little overprotective?"

He arched his brow. "Is that a question or a statement?"

"I guess a statement. My dad's job complicates my life," she said as she played with her hands.

Grady walked over and sat next to her on the couch. "Is your dad some high-profile person? Or is there another reason someone would want to kidnap you?"

"My dad is kind of a big deal back home."

Like a creepy stalker, he'd spent hours trying to find any information about her. He'd gotten her information off her dorm application. But Alida had to be the only person in college with absolutely no social media. It wasn't only her—it seemed that nobody in the town she came from had social media, either.

"What does your dad do?" He hadn't found anything about her parents, either. Their phone numbers and addresses weren't even online.

"He's the head of the council," she said, leaning closer to him.

"You mean like city commission?" he asked. The town she was from didn't even have a website.

She glanced away. "Yes."

"How long have you have had a bodyguard?"

Alida scoffed. "Boris has been my shadow since I was eight years old. At least now, I only have one. That took some major negotiations with my dad. Enough about my shadow and my dad. Why did you suddenly change your mind about talking to me? Was it because you were dating someone?"

Grady narrowed his eyes. "I have dated no one in a year," he murmured as he closed the distance between them. "You are the only person who has consumed all my thoughts for the last couple of months." He pushed a lock of hair behind her shoulder and traced her skin with his finger. Grady leaned forward and placed a kiss on the nape of Alida's neck, and she let out a moan. He kissed his way up and whispered in her ear, "You've been the star of all my fantasies."

He pulled back enough to angle her face and press his lips to hers. She gripped the back of his neck and pulled him closer. When his tongue passed over her lips, she opened her mouth. He wanted to pull her across his lap, but he ran his hands through her hair, pulling her closer.

Alida angled her face and nipped his bottom lip before pulling back. The kiss ended way too fast. But it was her eyes that caught him off guard. They'd turned from gray to light purple. He'd seen nothing so pretty before, but they changed the second she blinked.

Grady ran his hand down her face. "You are so pretty. But…"

"Don't even try taking it back. That kiss was amazing, and we have a great connection. Stop doing this hot-and-cold shit," she growled.

"I was going to say I shouldn't have taken advantage of you. Now you want to study, or should we watch a movie?"

She smiled. "Movie."

His phone beeped as they walked down the hall to the main common area. He glanced down at the text message: *Tonight.*

The text was from an unknown person, but he didn't need to see the name or the phone number to know who'd sent it. He figured more would come later, but he would spend as much time with Alida as he could until his mom fucked up his life again.

9

ALIDA

*S*he was very aware Grady was keeping something from her. The second his phone dinged, his back tightened, and he glared at the message. She didn't know if he would turn back into the distant person he'd been for the last few months, but she hoped he wouldn't. For the first time in a while, she felt settled. Not on edge. Not worried about the people trying to do sacrifices.

She'd overcome so many obstacles over the years to get here. It was her time to carve out her future and not worry about what anyone else needed or wanted. She knew she would work for the council, but this was her time to find her piece of happiness.

Grady's brown eyes searched hers. Alida wanted to know what the text said, but she felt like she wasn't trusting him at all if she used her powers to read his mind.

Grady tugged her hand until she was standing. When he twined his fingers with hers and walked to the sofa, she practically melted in his embrace. The night was perfect, but she wanted to know why he was an ass, because if she opened herself up too much, it would be a matter of time before he crushed her heart again. Breakups happened, but it was harder with someone who was her destiny.

He pulled her down next to him on the couch, and he wrapped his arms around her shoulder, pulling her in close. She rested her head on his shoulder.

"Can I ask you something?" she whispered.

"Sure." His body tensed.

"It shouldn't matter, but I need to ask why you were ignoring me for the last few months. I thought that night we watched a movie together, we had a connection. Still, the next day, you disappeared and turned into a total jackass."

He twined his fingers with hers and let out a slow breath. She wished for a second that she hadn't asked. She was worried he would tell her to leave. But she wanted to know what she'd done wrong. One second, everything was good between them, and the next, it was like he absolutely hated her. In class, he'd never called on her when she had the answer. Even when she needed help, it was always the professor to help her with her questions.

She should have been mad at him for the treatment, but after one look into his eyes earlier, all the worry had floated away. Alida watched as his tongue ran across his lips. She wanted to lean forward and kiss away the concern, but she also wanted answers.

"The morning after we watched a movie, I had a meeting with my mother." His eyes shot back to the table where his phone sat.

"Your dead mom?" She remembered the lie he'd told earlier. She could always tell when someone wasn't telling the truth. Calling him out for the lie had been on the tip of her tongue, but she didn't want him to stop talking to her again.

"Honestly, I wish she was dead. It would make my life so much easier, and for years, it was. When I was eight years old, my mom went to jail for trafficking large amounts of drugs. I spent most of my life in foster care. It wasn't bad, but it wasn't the best place in the world. My goal was to go to college and get a good job, leave the life I grew up behind. I had. I'm so close to getting to my goal."

Alida remained silent. She wanted to know his mother's name so her uncle Kai could grab information on her. Frankly, she didn't like the fact that Grady hadn't had a good childhood. Alida's parents had died, but she'd ended up with the best parents in the world. Every child deserved a happy childhood, but Alida knew they didn't always get it. "What is stopping you from your goal?"

"Nothing, until the morning after we'd watched *Transformation* together." Grady let out a long sigh. "My mother is now out of jail and came to find me. The message you heard earlier is from her again. She wants something. I'm worried about what will happen if I don't give her what she wants. Also, I was worried about her seeing you with me."

"Me?" Her parents had never worried about a human coming after her. Shifters or warlocks, yes. It made her fall a little more for him knowing he was trying to protect someone who could defend herself, along with having a bodyguard watching her ass often.

"I might not look very strong, but you don't have to worry about me. My dad and uncle have connections that can help you with your mom."

"Really?" Grady's brows drew together, and she knew she would figure out a way to help him.

She pressed her palm against his chest and ignored the electric current. "Yes, Uncle Kai can find anything, and I know he would help you if I asked. But you might not like what he finds. It could be bad."

"No, I don't trust her, and I'm not sure exactly what she is after."

"Okay...I'll call tomorrow."

"You barely know me, and you're going to ask your uncles to help me?"

She ran her tongue along her dry lips. "Yes, I know we haven't hung out much, but I have these feelings. Also, Uncle Kai loves playing on the dark web."

Grady turned and ran his fingers along her jawline. His touch lit a fire in her body. In the background, a

Christmas movie played, but her attention was only on Grady. He wrapped a muscular arm around her and pulled her close. She felt so petite in his arms as she rested her head under his chin. Everything felt right; the sadness from the last few months washed away. Her mom had always said she would fit perfectly in her mate's arms, and she did.

"Babe, you need to move."

Alida pulled back and stared into Grady's gray eyes. His pupils dilated. "Babe?" she asked, placing a kiss below his ear.

"I'm only holding back by a thread," he groaned.

"Maybe I don't want you to hold back."

"Do you know what you are saying?"

"Yes," she whispered.

Without hesitation, Grady pressed his mouth to hers, and he ran his tongue along the seam of her lips. With the one swipe, she was lost in his touch and her lips parted slightly. Grady groaned into her mouth as she ran her hands down his side, slipping under the hem of his black T-shirt. She loved the feel of his soft skin under her fingertips.

The kiss started out gentle. She melted into his hands as both their tongues tangled together. Everything in the world except them disappeared. She moved back a little so she could grip the bottom part of his shirt and tug it over his head.

Grady pulled back from the kiss and rested his forehead against hers. She used the opportunity to pull the shirt over his head. Her mouth watered as she wanted to run her tongue over his abs. She'd craved him for months, and now that she was with him, it was better than anything she fantasied about.

He pulled her up from the couch and ran his hands under her shirt, tugging it up. Grady tossed her shirt onto the sofa. She let out a sigh, remembering she was wearing her white lace bra and matching panties.

He unbuttoned her pants then kissed her stomach and hip as he slowly pulled down her pants. She was standing in the middle of the room with nothing on but her bra and panties. Alida's mouth went dry as he kissed the insider of her thigh. *Holly cow.*

"Grady," she groaned. Her legs shook with each touch of his lips, making it hard for her to stand. She placed her hand on his shoulder to keep herself from falling.

He pulled back. When he was standing, her fingers went to the button of his jeans, and she pulled down his jeans and boxers. Alida knelt next to him, nipping, licking as she worked her way down. Without warning, she wrapped her lips around his cock.

"Jesus, babe."

Grady ran his hands through her hair. She glanced up between her eyelashes and watched him tighten his jaw, keeping his composure. She took him deeper with wild abandonment. He tensed as she dragged her hands up his leg. And she wanted nothing more than to make him come.

"Alida," he gritted out. "You need to stop. I'm going to come."

Instead of stopping, she hummed and gripped his ass harder, keeping him close.

"Babe, you need to stop. When I come, I want to be deep inside you."

She didn't want to stop. This was the first time she had given a blow job, and she wanted Grady to enjoy it. She doubled her efforts until he reached down and pulled her up. His mouth pressed against her, his body smashed against hers. She could feel his hard cock against her stomach. The kiss was rough and demanding, unlike earlier. He walked her back to the bed until the back of her knees brushed against the covers. She lay in the middle of the bed and watched as Grady crawled next to her. *Holy hell, this man is perfect in every aspect.*

His finger ran along her hip, snagged the strap of her panties, and tugged them down her legs. He worked his way back up and kissed the inside of her leg. The touch of his soft lips against her skin sent a shiver down her body.

Grady's eyes locked with hers. "Touch yourself," he demanded.

Alida felt her cheeks burn as she dragged her fingers down her stomach and between her folds.

"Are you wet for me, babe?" Grady asked then pressed a kiss to the inside of her thigh.

"Yes." The word came out breathlessly.

Grady hummed against her clit. The vibration made her hips rise off the bed.

"Grady," she whispered, "I need…"

She didn't know what she needed. Bits of her magic sparked from her hand, and she closed her eyes to concentrate. If she didn't get herself under control, Grady would know something was strange.

Heat rushed down her spine, and he clasped his lips around her clit. His dark-blue eyes locked with hers. She only saw pure desire. When he pressed his fingers into her folds, her body ignited.

With each lick of his tongue, she was getting closer to the edge. She moved her hips to grind against his mouth. When he pressed into her folds harder, she ran her fingers through his hair.

She wasn't going to last much longer. Not with his hands all over her body. Desire coursed through her. She wanted more of everything, but mostly, she needed him inside her. Heat consumed her.

"Grady." His name came out breathlessly. She tugged at his hair.

He placed a kiss on the inside of her thigh. "Yeah, baby?" he asked then lowered his head one more time and sucked on her clit.

"I need you."

His lip twitched against her skin. "I'm right here." He pressed two fingers inside her. "You're so tight."

"I need more." Her hips bucked as he worked his fingers in and out, his lips pressed against her clit. She felt the rush of an orgasm. She gripped the bedspread as she went over the edge and screamed Grady's name.

Alida spread her legs wider as he continued to press his lips against her. It didn't take long before she felt the need to take over again. She squirmed under his touch, and when she thought she was about to go over the edge again, he stopped.

Grady rolled to the side and slid open the bedside drawer. He pulled out a condom, and she was glad one of them was thinking.

She watched as he tore the condom open with his teeth and slowly worked it down his hard length. Alida couldn't wait until he was buried deep inside her.

Grady leaned over and captured her nipple in his mouth as he ran his finger over her clit. She was lost in his touch as she pulled her over so that her leg straddled his thighs. Grady rested his hands on her hips as she reached between them and held him as she slowly worked her way down.

Her pussy convulsed around him as he went deeper inside her. Alida pressed her palms to his chest, waited for her to get used to him. He reached up and put her hair behind her ear. When their eyes connected, sparks ignited inside her. She had to break the connection, because it was too strong.

"Alida." Grady's hand rose from her hip, and he cupped her breast. She knew this was the start of something and hoped he wouldn't run when she had to explain the other world. But at this moment, the only thing that mattered was them. She knew life wouldn't always be easy, but she wanted to face it with Grady.

"Feels so good." She sighed as she rose and fell.

Grady pulled her close to his chest. Her breasts brushed against his skin as he flipped her onto her back. Grady surged forward and drove deep inside her. With each push, she felt the edge coming closer. Grady pressed his thumb to her clit and his lips to hers.

She couldn't hold back any longer as her body went over the edge at the same time as Grady's. Electricity flowed through her body, and a flash of light sparked in the room so quickly that she almost missed it. Alida knew it might be something she should worry about, but the only thing that mattered was them.

Grady rolled to the side and removed the condom before pulling her close. For a second, she let the blocks on her mind go, and it was silent. That was strange. She pushed a little harder, but Alida could no longer hear Grady's thoughts. And she loved it and worried all at the same time.

10

GRADY

*S*omething shifted. Grady didn't want to scare Alida and admit he could hear her heartbeat. There was no way mind-blowing sex would give him superpowers. But he couldn't explain why his hearing was extremely sensitive.

Alida rested her head on his chest, and he ran his hands through her hair, trying to figure out what to say. His mind raced back to the first day of class when she'd answered the question exactly like he was thinking. Then there was the incident where the TV channel had changed back and forth and the time the door had slammed in his face. Now he had super hearing. The only thing in common was Alida. Even if she had some supernatural power, he would never ask.

God, I'm losing my fucking mind. The term *mind-blowing sex* was the perfect way to explain what they'd had, because his mind had gone crazy. At least he'd had enough sense earlier to remember to grab a condom. He'd been so lost in her he'd almost forgot to use protection.

Grady scrubbed a hand over his face and let out a breath. They needed to discuss what had happened. One night with her wouldn't be enough, and he couldn't stand the idea that she might want to date someone else. "I'm not sure I'm going to let you leave the bed all weekend."

Alida turned and locked her gray eyes with his. They flickered almost purple for a second. "I'm not going to argue with that."

At that moment, his phone blared again. It was well past midnight, and he didn't want to answer the call.

Alida climbed out of bed and threw her shirt back on. "Why don't you take care of that, and I'm going to run and use the bathroom."

He knew she was giving him space to take the call. "I don't want to talk to her…" Grady glanced over at his phone. "And it feels like you just put up a wall between us." His phone finally stopped ringing, and he pulled her back into his arms. "See? No reason for you to go anywhere."

Then it started again.

"I'll be back soon. Take care of that." Alida pulled out of his arms and walked to the door. The loud ringing of his phone started again. He didn't remember turning his phone up that loud, but it made his ears hurt.

"What?" he growled into the phone. Grady didn't need to look at the number to know it was his mother calling.

"Is that any way to greet your mother?" she huffed.

"What do you want?" Grady asked.

"I wanted to see how my boy was doing."

"You don't have a motherly bone in your body. What do you need?" Grady wished his mother had never found him.

"There have been a couple delays on your dad's end. Next week, he's going to need your help."

Alida walked back into the room, and he forgot about the call for a second. His eyes went to her tight white shirt. *Damn, she is sexy.*

"Are you listening?" his mom screeched through the phone.

He had to pull it back because the volume of her voice made his ears ring. "No, something distracted me."

Alida smiled at him before placing a kiss on his cheek and sitting down on his bed. He needed to end the call so he could crawl in next to her. One taste wasn't enough—he wanted more.

"Well, son, I was saying your father is going to need your help next week. And if you want the money, you need to be there."

"You keep saying my father, but for years you told me he was dead." Grady paced back and forth. "Also, next week won't work for me."

Alida raised her brow, her gray eyes locked on Grady. She almost acted like she could hear the other side of the conversation—which would be nearly impossible unless his mother screamed.

"I thought he was dead as well. But that doesn't matter anymore. The only thing we need to worry about is getting half of the money he owes us."

God, she sounds like a scam artist.

"No." Nothing in life was free, and when it came to his mother, he knew it would only lead down a road he didn't want to go down. "I have plans."

"Really?" she asked. "Form my intel, you never leave your dorm except to go to school. And your school is out next week."

Alida's eyes narrowed, and she grabbed a piece of paper.

"Why do you have someone watching me?" he asked, stalling to see what Alida was writing. Grady already knew someone was watching him. He felt the hairs on the back of his neck raise every time he left his dorm.

She scribbled across the pad. She wanted him to go to West Virginia with him. There was no way he was pulling Alida into the mess. He shook his head. And that time, he didn't miss it. Her eyes turned a deep purple, and she pointed back to the page. The air in the room even became heavy.

Grady had so many questions, and none of them were for his mother, but he couldn't ask until he got her off the phone. "I'm spending the winter break in West Virginia. When I get back, I'll get the test."

"That's not good enough," his mother huffed.

A memory from his childhood flashed through his mind: his mother standing outside the local convenience store, making him beg for money while she flirted with every guy who walked by. And when he only got five dollars, she hit him across the head and told him it wasn't good enough. That hadn't stopped her from using the money to buy a pack of cigarettes.

"Well, he had the past three months to get what he needed," Grady reminded her. "So, no, I will not stick around and see what my supposed dad wants from me."

"You are the most ungrateful child." He could practically see her stomping her feet on the other end of the phone.

He might have wished for a family when he was younger, but he wasn't stupid enough to reconnect with his blood relatives now. "If what he needs is so important, he can come to West Virginia and get it from me. But I will not sit around and wait for a man I've never met. And I'm not even sure if you're telling me the truth. Does this guy even know I am his son? Or is this all some big scam?" Grady was leaning toward it being a scam.

"He's real, and he owes me. Don't you forget, you also owe me for the time I spent in jail? It's all your fault. If you hadn't wined so much, the protective custody people would've never shown up to the house."

There was no way he was going to have the same conversation again. He'd already had this fight with her and knew she would only see it from her way. "You have my number. Call when you have more information."

Many of the kids in foster care with him had dreamed of meeting their fathers or mothers. Some had wondered how they ended up in the system. Grady, though, had known it was his mom, and she'd only said hateful things about his father. Still, he always wondered if she even knew who his dad was. Grady knew one thing, though: he didn't care to meet his dad, even if it meant enough money to help him get on his feet. He'd learned early in life that everything came with a price tag.

"Or you could spend your winter break getting to know your mother better. We've been apart for so many years."

His mother could shift from a crazy bitch to a person in need within seconds. The act had fooled him when he was a kid, but now, he saw through it. He didn't trust her. Hell, there wasn't anyone he actually trusted anymore. "Not my problem. I need to go."

"Hold on, Grady," she begged, and the phone went silent for a second. "I know I'm not the best mother…"

Grady huffed. "That's an understatement."

She ignored his comment and continued. "I have…

Doesn't matter. All that I care about is making sure you are okay. I'm doing this to help you and would really like to spend some time with you."

Grady ran his hand over his face and sat down on the bed next to Alida. She pressed her palm to his thigh, and it grounded him. Just being near her helped him think more clearly. His mom is a con artist, and he wouldn't fall for her tricks again.

"I'll talk to you soon." Grady disconnected, and he let out a long sigh.

"Thanks for the cover story," Grady said.

"Oh, it's not a cover story. You're coming home with me for winter break. And whatever your mom is planning, my uncle can help."

"I'm not dragging you or your family into my fucked-up situation," Grady said, twining their fingers together.

"My uncle can help. It's kind of what my family does."

"I thought your dad worked for the local government?" Grady asked.

"Winter Haven is a different type of town. It's not easily explained."

"Like how your eyes flash purple really quick, or the air turns thick when you get mad. Let's not forget about the TV turning by itself." He sounded like a mental case saying all the strange things that had happened since meeting her. At least he didn't mention that he thought she'd read his mind. Maybe he should, then she wouldn't want anything to do with him.

"Everything has a reasonable explanation," she said without looking him in the eye.

"So you don't think I'm crazy for saying anything I just said?"

"There are so many things in the world we can't explain. You saw *Transformation*, and look what that little girl could do."

Grady threw his head back and laughed. Alida was staring at him dead on, like it wasn't a joke. "That was a movie. Thanks for a laugh. If your parents are okay with me coming, I'll go home with you. But you need to let them know about the danger."

"My last final is on Thursday."

"Then we can head out on Friday. Everyone needs to be out of the dorms Friday night. I can have Tom look over the floor for me." Grady was excited and nervous. Things were going fast with Alida, but he also didn't want to spend any time away from her. He was about to lean forward to capture her lips when someone knocked on his door.

He let out an aggravated sigh and threw open the door. On the other side stood the kid from a few doors down. He wore a pair of jeans and T-shirt with a heavy metal band on it. Grady hadn't seen him much since the day he'd moved in.

"I'm locked out of my room."

"Okay." Grady turned to grab the master keys when the kid stepped into his room.

"God, she has a nice pair of tits on her. I would totally hit that."

Grady turned toward the kid, ready to knock out his front teeth. "What the fuck did you say?"

The kid took a step back and bumped into the door, holding up his hands. "Dude, I said nothing. I just need my dorm unlocked."

Grady glanced over at Alida, and she shrugged. "I heard nothing."

"Dude needs to be hitting that more. Maybe he wouldn't be so stressed out."

"I swear to God, you better apologize."

"Dude, I don't know what you're talking about."

Grady opened his mouth and shut it. Something was truly going wrong with him. He followed the guy to his room and unlocked the door.

"Thanks, man," the guy grumbled before shutting his door.

Grady passed a freshman in the hall, and she winked at him. "I would sleep with that piece of meat in a quick second." But her mouth didn't move.

I've genuinely lost my mind.

11

ALIDA

"Hey, Mom!" Alida said.

She'd hooked her phone up to Grady's car the second they were on the interstate. For the first hour, they'd listened to music, but then her cellphone had cut to her mom's call. Worry filled her stomach for a second. She hadn't told her family she was bringing Grady home with her.

"Where are you?" Talia asked. "I thought you would be here by now!"

Grady glanced at her with a raised eyebrow. She couldn't exactly tell her mom that she couldn't transport home because she was bringing a human along for the holiday vacation.

Today was the first day she'd seen Grady since Thanksgiving weekend. They'd both been busy with finals, and he'd had TA work. With so much going on, she'd also forgotten to call and tell her parents about

Grady. Well, that wasn't one hundred percent true. She didn't want her dad to ask questions.

"I'm driving back with Grady and decided not to take the flight. I'm surprised Boris didn't tell you we were driving since I see his car three spots back."

Grady's eyes flashed to the rearview mirror, and his perfect lips dipped down. His hands gripped the steering wheel tighter as he sped down the interstate.

"Oh…is this the human you were talking about?" Talia asked.

Before she had time to reply, her dad's voice came across the line. "You're bringing a human home, Alida?"

Alida let out a sigh and pinched the bridge of her nose. "FYI, you guys are on speakerphone. The human can hear everything you are saying." She laughed, hoping Grady didn't think they were unusual.

Her dad ignored what she said. "I need his first name, last name, and date of birth. It would help Kai out if you could give me a social security number as well." Kirin's voice boomed through the compact car.

Alida closed her eyes and rested her head against the headrest.

Grady cleared his throat. "Grady Carson, date of birth is May sixteenth, nineteen ninety-six. If Alida's uncle is as good as she said, he doesn't need my social security number. Alida was supposed to tell you I was coming. Especially since my mother is causing me issues. I can drop Alida off and head back to DC."

"No," Kirin growled. "I trust my daughter. But I'm

still going to research your life. Also, if you are in danger, our home is the safest place you can be. If she thinks you need help, Kai and I are the best to get that done."

"I don't want to put your family in harm's way or make any of the citizens upset with you."

Kirin chuckled. "Citizens? What did Alida tell you I do for a living?"

"A local commissioner or mayor for the town. But I would like to let you know it's almost impossible to find any information about Winter Haven. I looked everywhere. It's like the town doesn't exist. Not sure that is a very good way to get people to move there."

"We don't want people moving here," Kirin grumbled.

Grady's brown eyes locked with hers for a second. She would need to explain the whole supernatural world sooner or later. But she had no clue how to. It wasn't like she could shift into an animal. Nope. She couldn't even read Grady's mind anymore. But she needed to tell him before her brother transformed into a dragon.

"We are happy for you to come to visit," Talia said. "And I'll make sure Uncle Kai and Lucy are here. Is there anything else you need to tell us?"

"Nope, thanks, Mom," Alida said before disconnecting the call.

"Human?"

"It's just something my dad says." It sounded like the

lamest excuse, but she couldn't come up with anything else in the brief notice.

"Is there anything else you want to tell me about your family before we get there? Because I like you, Alida, and I want to make this work."

"Just be yourself." She sighed. "And keep an open mind. My family is a little different. You'll get along with my dad just fine. He can be a little intimidating, but he's like a giant cuddle bear."

"I remember your dad the day you moved in. He seemed very intimidating."

"That's just how he acts to the outside world. But he's protective of the people inside his close circle." Alida wasn't ready to explain to Grady that he was her mate and her father would do anything to help him. But hopefully, during his time with her family, she would figure out a way to explain everything.

"Did your family always live in West Virginia?"

"Mostly yes," Alida told Grady. She couldn't tell him her dad was over three hundred years old and lived all over the world. It was easier saying her family always lived there. "My dad's family founded the town."

"Is that why he's on the commission?"

The more questions he asked, the more lies she had to tell. Alida hated lying, but she didn't know how to explain her life yet. "When I was younger, the town had a corrupt leader. Once he was taken down...I mean removed from office, my dad and uncles worked to clean up the community."

"Have you thought about politics and going down the same path as your dad?"

"Yes, I would love to work with my dad one day. I think my undergrad in psychology will help. I have a certain ability to read people," Alida said. "My aunt wants me to follow in her footsteps and go to medical school. She's a world-renowned scientist. Over the last ten years, she's isolated parts of human DNA to figure out what causes cancer."

"You never mentioned what your mom does," Grady said, glancing in the rearview mirror.

Boris 's black SUV was still following them. He no longer tried to hide the fact he was behind them, but Alida didn't mind the extra security.

"She works with Dad. Mom is his sounding board when dealing with the tough calls. They make an impressive pair, and since Dad took over, things have calmed down."

"Your small town had that much crime?"

Crime would have been a simple fix. The past few months had brought many memories from the past she wished she didn't have to remember. And some made her sad. The fact that she no longer saw her real mother's ghost had bothered her lately. "It did. But know it's better."

"We're going to have to stop soon and get gas."

Alida pulled up the location of the closest gas station on her phone and directed Grady where to go.

When they turned off the interstate, Boris turned as well, not too far behind.

While Grady filled the gas tank, Alida ran into the store to buy more snacks for the road. She'd already eaten the package of licorice and a bag of chips. Her hands were full, and as she placed everything on the counter, the cashier raised his brow at the massive amount of junk food she was buying.

The bell over the door chimed as two men walked through. Alida didn't pay them much attention as she paid and waited for the cashier to bag her food. When she was back in the car, Grady frowned toward the store, watching the two men who had walked in while she was paying.

"Did they say something to you?"

Grady eyed them a second longer before turning toward her. His eyes were wide. "You wouldn't believe me if I told you."

"You would be surprised," Alida answered.

Grady drummed his fingers on the steering wheel.

Alida glanced in the rearview mirror and saw that Boris was watching the men in the store as well. They were at the counter, paying. "It seems you and Boris have an issue with those men. Do we need to call the cops or ditch them?"

"Ditch them."

A smile spread across her face. That was something she could do. For years, she'd ditched her bodyguard. That was one of the few things her father taught her but wished he hadn't. "Okay, start the car, and we will lose them."

Without questioning her, Grady started the car and pulled onto the interstate.

"Now press your foot down and gain some ground."

Grady did as she said, but he was only going ten miles over the speed limit.

"Have you never outrun someone or had to lose a tail?" Alida huffed.

"Never had a reason to lose a tail. Also, don't want to get a speeding ticket."

Alida sat back in the seat and shook her head. With each mile they drove, she watched in the rearview mirror. He still hadn't told her why they were ditching the men in the store. He looked nervous that she wouldn't believe him. Her mom always said communication was the key to a successful relationship.

Boris flashed his lights behind her. He was signaling for them to turn off the highway.

"Take the next exit."

Grady slowed down.

"Don't let everyone know where we are going. Speed back up. Yes, we probably lost them, but to make sure, go faster."

Grady huffed and turned off the road. Besides Boris and them, the side road was deserted.

"So, you going to finally tell me what you saw or heard?"

He glanced over at her with worry in his eyes. "The guy was thinking of ways to run us off the road."

"Thinking?" Alida turned her full attention to him. "Like you read his mind?"

Well, this makes things a lot more interesting. She racked her brain, thinking back to the first night they'd slept together and how strange he'd acted toward the student who was locked out. That was the same night she could no longer read his thoughts. "When did you start reading people's minds?"

Grady glanced to the side and stared for a second. "You should be freaked out by the fact I heard someone's thoughts. Believe me, it's not something I wanted or like."

Alida winced inwardly. She hadn't known that would happen. It had taken years for her to learn to control her mind-reading powers. Sometimes she still couldn't control it if the person was thinking too hard. "Let's stop at the next diner, and we can talk all of this out. But until we get there, let's say I don't think you're crazy and I want to know what those men were after."

"You."

Well, that wouldn't be the first time someone was after her, but her parents usually had a warning first. "Okay, and they wanted to get a ransom?"

Grady's knuckles turned white as he gripped the steering wheel tighter. "No, he thought you were hot and wanted...It doesn't matter what he thought. But he needed to turn you over to some doctor about your

DNA. God, saying this shit out loud sounds even worse."

Having someone after her DNA sounded terrible. That hadn't been an issue for years. Too many things were happening lately—the stupid movie about Kael and the people killing themselves for a sacrifice. Now someone was after her DNA. "Look. Over there is a diner."

It would make do as a place to talk things out, because she did not want to tell him about her powers while he was driving.

"You want me to pull in to a diner from a horror movie?"

Alida rolled her eyes. "The parking lot is partially full. It can't be that bad. Maybe we're about to find a hidden gem. Pull around back, so our car isn't facing the road."

"Or we're about to die in a diner in the middle of nowhere," Grady said as he parked next to the dumpster behind the restaurant.

12

GRADY

*A*lida hadn't acted very surprised when he told her he'd heard someone's thoughts. Instead, she'd coached him on how to lose a tail. He still wasn't sure that was the best idea, because someone was clearly following them. But now they sat across from each other in a booth at the back of the restaurant, next to an exit—another thing Alida had insisted on.

Grady hadn't gotten used to the voices he was hearing, and he couldn't figure out why he couldn't hear a single thought of Alida's. In this case, he might be better off. She could very well think he was insane.

"Are you going to tell me why you aren't freaking out?" he asked Alida and waited for her to set down the sticky plastic menu.

Her gray eyes connected with his, and she let out a long sigh. "I don't know where to start. On a scale from one to ten, how freaked out are you by the voices?"

That was a little less since she seemed to think it was expected as well. "Solid fifteen."

"Really? That's a little overdramatic."

The bell on the front door chimed. Alida's bodyguard walked through, and she waved to him before turning back to Grady. He had to give her bodyguard credit. Alida had sent him on a wild-goose chase before telling him to pull into the back parking lot of the rundown diner. Even her bodyguard faced the door when he sat down and watched the surroundings.

"Where are you on this scale?" Grady countered.

He didn't miss the worry that crossed over Alida's face. "What if I told you the movie *Transformation* is actually real?" Her question almost came out as a whisper.

Grady thought back to the movie. The special effects were really well done. Did he think people could turn into dragons? No. But he'd never expected to hear someone's thoughts, either. His mind went to the little girl in the movie. Everyone complained that she could read their minds. And Alida had hated when he'd said the girl was unbelievable. But he would not admit out loud that the movie didn't sound as far-fetched anymore.

"Do you think the movie is true?" Grady asked, and Alida's eyes flickered around the diner before she nodded. "How much of the movie do you think is real?"

Fucking hell. I might not be losing my mind. Is Alida the reason I can hear other people's thoughts? Grady was always open to the world of science. On a level, he believed in psychics, but he thought it was something they were born with.

"Most of it is true. The part that isn't is mostly around Kael. That dude was pure evil and the scum of the supernatural world." Alida let out a breath. "So you don't look one hundred percent convinced the supernatural world exists. When the server comes over, read her mind, and I will too."

Grady didn't have time to ask a follow-up question as an older woman walked up to the table and scowled at Alida. "What would you like?"

"I'll have the steak special, rare, fries, and a Coke."

He took a moment to read the woman's thoughts. "The supernatural princess should know better than to bring a human into a shifter restaurant." Grady wondered what the fuck was going on, but the woman growled at him.

"What do you want?" She wasn't friendly at all toward him like she'd been to Alida a second ago.

"The same is fine."

She eyed him for a second before she turned and walked over to Boris's booth and took his order.

Alida closed her eyes for a second. "She didn't like that I brought a human into a shifter place. Mind you, it's not like I knew that when we pulled in. But I think this whole community is shifters. So if those people are after me, we might not have much time to figure everything out. So you're going to have to catch on real quick."

Grady glanced over at Boris , who was watching the door like a hawk. Grady was sure he was losing his mind, but if they were in danger, he would need to snap out of it quick.

"Okay, so you can read minds as well. But how did I all of a sudden start? Is this like a disease you passed through sex?"

Alida's eyes flashed purple for a second, and Grady couldn't help but wince from his words. Maybe he shouldn't have said he'd caught a disease.

"No, you can't catch my powers from sex. I've never heard anything so stupid in my life before."

Well, he'd never thought people had powers before, but he would not dig his hole any deeper. "Okay, so how did I magically start hearing things."

Alida bit her lip for a second. "I'm going to have to have my aunt take a sample of your blood, and she can figure out why."

Damn. Another person who wants my blood. But at least he knew why Alida's aunt planned to run tests. He still wasn't sure what his biological dad would want with his DNA.

"So can you do anything else besides reading minds?"

Without saying anything, she opened her hand. The air around him felt like a hot, humid day in Florida. The air was so thin, it made it hard to breathe. The fork on his side of the table flashed across the tabletop and ended up in her hands.

"So you can do magic tricks," Grady responded, not quite ready to admit that he'd seen her drag the fork across the table without using her hand.

"I have magical abilities, but I don't like to use the magic," she told him. "At times, it can go a little out of control."

Grady shook his head but kept his question to himself as the server set down their salads. "There are people in this town who don't like you."

The statement had been directed at Alida. Grady wanted to grab Alida by the hand and rush out of the place. He needed to get her to her parents' house before something terrible happened.

"We should just go," he said.

"I'm different in the supernatural world. Many people who don't know me fear me. It's nothing we have to worry about. Even the bad guys who will be here soon. I didn't want to take them on at the gas station because it would be difficult," Alida muttered like this was an everyday occurrence.

"Why do they not like you?" The thought of someone not liking Alida made his blood boil.

"I'm different. Also, everyone in this room is a shifter. From the scent, most are feline. I would guess mountain lions. Boris is the only wolf shifter in the place. I think the guy at the counter in a flannel shirt and jeans, sipping on a coffee—he's a grizzly bear."

Alida watched him, probably trying to figure out how much he was going to freak out. The idea of someone shifting into a bear or a wolf sounded crazy. She'd turned his entire world upside down the day he'd seen her in the hall.

"*Transformation* is based on my family. The little girl is me."

Grady nodded, not sure what to say. He hadn't said the nicest things about the little girl. Now it made sense why she'd stuck up for the girl so much.

"So, that means your dad is a dragon?" He laughed, thinking that was the part of the movie she'd said was untrue. The part where Kael turned humans into shifters bothered him a little.

"Yes, my dad is also the head of the West Virginia Council. The reason you couldn't find anything about our town was because we don't want humans visiting or living there."

Well, that made sense. The idea of her dad being a dragon freaked him out. At the most, he'd feared her dad might have a gun, but a transformation into a giant dragon was another thing. Their conversation with her dad in the car earlier made sense. He called him a human.

"You've thrown a lot of information at me. I'm still waiting for you to say, 'Gotcha!' Instead, you keep acting normal." He really wanted her to say it was a joke.

She tilted her head to the side. "Honestly, I knew

something was different about you the first day we met. Supernatural people...well, it's hard to explain, and we don't have time to go over that part. Until we had sex, I could read your mind. Now you're the only person on the earth I can't read. My family is harder to read because they've learned over the years how to block their thoughts."

"Is there a way not to hear everything?" Grady had heard more than he ever wanted to know about the students in his class. It'd made taking his finals a nightmare. Some students would think of the problems in their heads. A few of the students didn't know what they were doing, and his statistics teacher had pictured the women in the class naked. Grady had also learned he was sleeping with his T.A. Since Grady knew for sure that he wasn't losing his mind, he planned to email the dean of the college when he got to Alida's parents' house.

"Yes, and no. Sometimes thoughts are too loud to block out, but most, you can. When someone is upset, their thoughts seem to come out louder. These are things I can teach you about at my parents' hou—" Alida's eyes turned white.

Grady reached across the table and grabbed her hand. He looked over to Boris, and he just watched her, not moving. Grady had no clue what to do. It seemed as though time slowed for a second. When he went to stand, she tightened her grip on his hand and blinked a couple times.

"What the fuck, Alida?"

"You watched the movie. I get visions of the future sometimes. One just happened."

"Are we going to die?" Grady felt like that was a very valid question.

She rolled her eyes. "I can't see anything connected to my future. Only others. Seems I can't see anything connected to yours either. But our server needs help."

As if on cue, she walked back to the table with the bill. Alida grabbed the women's hand. "See that man over there?" She nodded toward Boris. "He can help you with your problem."

The woman went to protest. "You know who I am. That man over there might annoy me, but he is a good man and can help you. Tell him Alida saw it. He'll know what that means."

She nodded and walked to the table, holding Boris's bill. When she spoke to him, he glanced at Alida, and she nodded.

"What did you just do?"

"Like I said, I saw a glimpse of the future. If she stays with the man she's with, he will kill her. Boris can help her. Some shifters have a violent tendency. Not all, but the man she's with does. I just found a way to help her."

He kept falling more and more for Alida every minute he was with her. The whole reading minds and the shifting thing was a lot for him to take in, but she made it seem so much easier. "God, that is sexy."

"Me chowing down on a sixteen-ounce steak?" Alida asked, popping the last piece into her mouth.

"No, using your gift to help others."

Alida shrugged and glanced toward the front of the diner. "Okay, so the bad guy followed us here. I think we make a run for it out the back before they get to close. Boris will have his hands full watching over the waitress as well."

"But isn't he your bodyguard?"

Rather than respond, Alida jumped out of the booth and grabbed his hand. Thankfully, the exit was only steps away. The emergency exit had a huge red bar advertising the alarm. Grady tried to warn Alida before she pushed through. But the alarm didn't sound. He sighed as he stood next to her, only fifty feet from his car. Alida scanned the lot and stopped him from moving forward. The smell of shifter was thick in the back parking lot. It hadn't been there when they'd first arrived, so she knew something was wrong.

"Do you have an auto-lock on your keys?"

He nodded.

She held out her hands. "Let me see them." They were both still covered by the dumpster outback. Alida pointed his fob toward his car and hit the unlock button.

His car exploded, sending a blast of heat at them. The force of the explosion knocked them back against the wall of the diner. They both slid to the ground. Ash marred Alida's face, and Grady's ears were ringing.

"What the fuck?" he yelled.

"Bomb!" she yelled back at him. "Do you trust me?"

For some reason he didn't understand, he did trust her. He nodded, but before he could ask a follow-up question, she grabbed his hand. Then they disappeared.

13

ALIDA

*O*ver the years, Alida had perfected her landing at home. Her parents knew not to move furniture without telling her, because it would cause a mess.

Alida and Grady crashed down onto the Christmas tree. Sparkly silver bulbs rolled across the floor. Grady had pink tinsel in his hair. Water spilled from the Christmas tree stand. Her ears still ringing from the blast in the parking lot, Alida looked around the room, seeing if she'd messed up. Nope, her parents had moved the Christmas tree.

Her mother stood in the living room, a hand over her mouth. Kirin pinched his brow.

"You pick this year to move the Christmas tree?" Alida asked as she tried to get up. But tree sap stuck her hand to the floor.

Grady looked like he was about to puke. It wasn't

uncommon for transportation to make someone sick the first time. He sat next to her on the destroyed Christmas tree, his head resting in his hands.

"You said you were driving home," her mother murmured, walking over to help her up. With a gloved hand, Talia helped her stand, while Kirin helped Grady get to his feet.

Alida followed her mom and dad into the open kitchen. It wasn't until they were standing by the island did she notice the gash on the side of Grady's head.

"You're hurt." Alida grabbed a rag from the drawer and held it under the running water. Her parents hadn't said a word, only watched her. Alida's mother already understood that she'd found her mate. And it didn't take her father long to catch on. She wasn't sure how he felt about it, and at the moment, the only thing that mattered was fixing Grady.

"It's only a scratch. Can we talk about the fact that someone blew up my car, and you transported us? You fucking transported me, Alida. Nowhere in our conversation earlier did you say transportation was a thing. All you said was 'Do you trust me?' I thought you had some badass way to take the men down. One moment we were about to fight, and the next, I was lying on top of a Christmas tree. My stomach feels like I rode a rollercoaster twenty times and wasn't smart enough to get off."

Kirin's lip ticked up. "You get used to the feeling after a while. I'm surprised how well you're taking all of this. You know if you tell a single human, I will have my men kill you."

Alida pressed her hand on Grady's shoulder until he sat down on the chair. She used the wet cloth to clean the red gash on the side of his face. "He won't have you killed. Because Grady will not tell anyone." She glanced at her parents for a second. "Um, Grady developed the ability to read minds."

Both of her parents stared at her for a second. Neither of them asked how he'd developed the power. She wasn't ready to admit to her parents that she'd had sex with Grady.

Kirin's eyes flashed orange for a second. "You're not mated."

"Mated?" Grady asked.

They had so many things to talk about, but she still didn't know where to start. At least he hadn't run for the door or tried to call the police. The police in her hometown wouldn't have done anything anyway. They were funded by the council, and everyone on the force was a shifter.

"I'll explain later. No, we aren't mated. Can we just say his powers developed around me? I'm not really up to discussing when it occurred."

Her dad growled, "We can go over to Lucy's and Kai's. Maybe we should go right now. The kids are already over there."

Her parents stood next to her and touched her forearm.

Alida glanced at Grady. "You ready?"

His eyes widened. "Hell no! Don't you guys have a car? I still don't under—"

She didn't wait for him to finish. Alida smiled and grabbed his hand. Transportation took only seconds. They landed in the middle of the kitchen. This time, she was clear.

Grady turned and ran for the door. He barely made it to the lawn before he puked. Alida winced, knowing he was sick because of her. It took time to get used to her powers. The more people transported with her, the less sick they felt. Doing two quick transports had drained some of her energy.

She followed him outside, sat down on the grass next to him, and placed her hand on his back. "The drive to Uncle Kai's house takes a while. Also, I thought if I caught you off guard, it wouldn't be as bad."

Grady wiped his mouth and sat next to her. His face was white, and his pupils were dilated. Lucy would have something to help him feel better.

"I would like to go on the record saying I hate teleportation."

Her lip ticked. "Noted, but if you're in danger, I will use it."

She would do anything to keep Grady safe, even if that made him sick for a few minutes. His color was already returning. They sat for a few minutes in silence. Her uncle's back yard overlooked the valley of the mountain. It was so peaceful. She'd missed that over the past few months. She didn't need to keep her guard up or work to not hear other people's voices.

Grady broke the silence. "How can I stop hearing other people's thoughts? Before we transported, I heard about fifty different ways your dad plans on killing me. We could've kept it a secret about my powers. He figured out really quick we slept together, and he isn't pleased."

"Lucy's going to figure out why it happened. Yes, humans have gotten powers, but only after they mated. We didn't officially mate."

"What do you mean by 'mate'?"

Movement to the side of the yard caught her attention. Her brother, sister, and cousins were watching them. She also knew they were using their shifter hearing to listen to every word she and Grady said. Since she didn't use her powers very often, Alida hoped she wasn't about to blow up Grady and herself. She closed her eyes and called to the magic deep in her soul. With a wave of her hand, she made a bubble.

When Alida opened her eyes, Grady was poking at the colorful outer shell. It reminded her of a bubble she'd played with when she was a kid. But Grady poking his finger at the structure did nothing. She opened her mind to see if she could hear her siblings. Kyle's lips moved, but she couldn't hear a word they said. It was peaceful.

"We had an audience. Now nobody can hear us, and you shouldn't have to hear anyone's thoughts. Before we get into the mate thing or how to stop hearing other people, how are you doing?"

Grady ran his hand through his hair. "I think okay. Not sure why I'm not freaked out more. Maybe I'm having a delayed reaction, and it will all hit me later."

Alida tilted her head to the side. "I've heard fate never pairs someone with a person who can't handle what will happen. It's not often a supernatural is paired with a human. But I'm wondering if you have some shifter or supernatural DNA dormant in your body. When my parents mated, my dad didn't develop the ability to read a person. My mom got his immortality."

"Wait, immortality? Like, live forever?"

"Yes, my dad is part of a line of immortal dragons. Their mates can live as long as they do. Most shifters live a very long life. I'm not sure how long my lifespan will be because when my DNA was made in a lab, they constructed me out of many people. There is a huge possibility I'm immortal."

Grady stared at her, blinking.

She was losing him. "We're getting ahead of ourselves. Some shifters are immortal. Does that bother you?"

"Honestly, I don't know. Can we start with the ability to block people's thoughts?"

She nodded, and for the next half hour, Alida worked with Grady, teaching him how to find his powers and lock them away in his mind. The best way was to build a box in his mind and shove the powers deep into it. At first, it would take lots of concentration, but over time, it would become second nature. Then his powers would only come out when he wanted to use them. There was still the issue of people with loud thoughts, but few were.

"I wish I would've learned this after I started hearing people," Grady grumbled. "I still can't believe they blew up my car. Still don't quite understand why we didn't call the police or someone."

It would take a while for Grady to understand the supernatural world. Guilt washed over her for a second. He was now wrapped into her dangerous world because of her. Was it selfish of her to want to keep him as her mate when he would be in danger?

Off in the distance, a large object and a small object came into sight. She knew it was her uncle Conley. There was a good chance Nyx was on his back, and Zack flew next to them. She hoped Grady wasn't about to freak out. He looked up into the sky as the enormous dragon flew over them and landed on the second-story balcony of the lair. That was where Kai kept extra clothes for everyone.

Grady turned to her. "You just saw two dragons, right?"

"Yep."

"And someone was sitting on the large dragon?"

"That's Aunt Nyx. My mom rides on Dad, and he gives us rides whenever we ask. I'm sure he would give you one."

He nodded, lay back on the lawn, and looked up at the sky. "You understand this is a lot to take in, right? As for the ride, no thank you. It would be the perfect chance for your dad to drop me from the sky."

"He wouldn't. If you want, we can leave, but we have the people after me, and we also have the issue with your mom."

Alida worried Grady's mother knew something deeper about him. *Why else would she want his DNA? Especially after he developed abilities.* Over the years, Alida had spent enough time in Lucy's lab to know that abilities didn't just happen. Most of the time, the person had shifter DNA as well.

"I think it's safer to stay here. That's saying a lot, because I had to listen to how your dad wanted to stick me in a field and light it on fire. Then eat the ash. To make sure I was dead."

She couldn't hold back the laughter. "My dad wouldn't ever do that. He knows what a mate means. Also, he wouldn't want to make me upset. Things happen when I get too mad."

"Like what?"

The west side of her parents' house was newer. When she was going through her teenage years, she wasn't always the best behaved. Talia telling her she had to stay home hadn't always gone over well. Once, her anger overtook her, and she'd ended up blowing up the side of the house. The incident still hadn't gotten her what she'd wanted, and they'd grounded her for months.

"Doesn't really matter. Also, those things my father thought—he did that because he knew you could hear his thoughts. One thing I know is he would do anything to protect you. My family means the world to me, and I would never bring someone here who could hurt them, and they know this."

Grady pulled Alida closer, and she rested her head on his chest. They lay in peace for a while until she looked up, and her dad was staring down, saying something. She smiled and placed her hand to her ear, indicating that she couldn't hear him. He rolled his eyes and motioned for her to drop the ward.

Once the ward was down, they were no longer locked in her bubble, and Alida could hear the chatter of the birds and the world again.

"We need to head to the lair. Kai thinks he has some information, and Lucy wants to play with her new science project."

14

GRADY

*G*rady wasn't sure he enjoyed being referred to as a science project. But they needed answers, and staying in Alida's bubble wasn't an option. Alida and Grady followed Talia and Kirin through the house and into the garage.

"I thought we were heading to a lab. Not sure if I want my blood drawn in the garage," Grady grumbled.

The place looked clean—three black cars were parked on the white marble floor. Grady was sure all the cars had cost well over a hundred thousand dollars.

Alida rolled her eyes. "This is the entrance to Uncle Kai's secret lair."

Grady burst out laughing, thinking she was making a joke. But nobody laughed. Everyone stared at him like he'd lost his mind. Any sane person would run for the door and not look back. But Grady waited for what happened next, and it didn't take long.

Kai flipped a switch on the wall, and the center black sports car rose into the air. Everyone but Grady walked under it. Kai placed his hand on the ground, and a computer screen came up and scanned the room. After a moment, a piece of the floor slid open. Talia, Kirin, and Kai walked down.

Alida took his hand and pulled him toward the open hole in the floor. With each step down the narrow staircase, he took in his surroundings. His fingers ran against the gold-plated wall. The place had to cost a small fortune. Grady had never asked what Kai did for a living. He knew his wife was a scientist, but gold walls seemed like something a billionaire would do.

When they finally reached the end of the staircase, they were all in a small room. The only way out was the way they had just come.

Grady jumped when a voice came through the loudspeaker. "Welcome to our home, Grady."

Alida rolled her eyes. "That's Uncle Kai's second wife. Except she's a computer. I think we're on version 19.4. Mostly because the first few versions kept wanting to kill Lucy."

"I never wanted Lucy dead. Only to know her place."

Kai winced. "Even after years of tweaking, she still has a deep affection for me."

"Because you built a girlfriend," Kirin muttered. "One you should've gotten rid of years ago. Well, don't get me wrong. I love how she cooks and does my taxes, but she's a little too much in love with you."

Kai shrugged and placed his hand on the wall, and a gold elevator appeared.

Grady leaned over and whispered in Alida's ear, "Why is everything gold?"

It seemed a little over-the-top for the entrance to someone's lair. He assumed Kai wasn't inviting everyone over to party in the secret location since it took so much work to get down there.

"Dragon's like gold." Alida shrugged like it was something he should have known.

He'd seen in movies and books how dragons loved gold and jewels, but her uncle seemed to be taking it to an extreme. He wanted to joke back and ask where the cave was, but he bit his tongue.

Grady twined his fingers with Alida's as the elevator dropped quickly. The door swung open, and he expected a dark cave with more gold, but it was the total opposite. Windows lined the far wall. The floor was white marble, and a gold table in the center of the room held a vase of roses.

"Wow."

Alida turned to him. "It's pretty incredible. Wait until you see Lucy's lab."

They walked down a long hallway. Kai went into a room halfway down. But Alida kept pulling Grady until they came to a stop at the end. They stepped inside the lab, and a small woman with blond hair stared at a tube of blood. Next to her, a little girl in a lab coat sat on the counter.

When they stepped into the lab, she turned around and smiled. "This is so exciting. Why don't you come over here and have a seat in the chair?" The woman practically bounced on her tiptoes.

Grady wondered if this was still the best idea. But Alida dragged him across the room. She patted his arm before pushing him into the chair. For being so small, she had a lot of strength. Alida jumped up onto the table next to him. Grady kept his eyes on the scientist as she rushed around the lab's collection of large needles and test tubes. He agreed to a test of his blood, but it looked like she was going to do hours of experiments on him.

"Can we talk about what you are looking for in my blood?" Grady asked, hoping that would stop her from grabbing another syringe from the drawer.

"Oh. These aren't only for you. I'm going to test Alida, too. Since this happened after you guys"—she glanced at her daughter—"had S.E.X."

Alida rolled her eyes. "We knew what you meant. But I went through your pokes for years. You have enough of my blood to build your own person. Not saying you should do that. Athena is crazy enough for this house."

"I heard that, Alida. It's not nice to speak ill of someone when they can hear you."

Lucy placed the items on the table next to them. "If

Grady's DNA changed after you did the down and dirty—"

"Eww. Please don't say that again."

"Your DNA might've changed. And we know every time your DNA changes, you get another power. Has anything changed on your front?"

Alida winced. Grady hadn't even thought something might change for her. He was so stuck in his own head. *God, why didn't I think of that? Well, probably because everything that happened in the last week was so unbelievable.*

Alida sighed and held out her arm. "My magic feels closer to the surface, and I can't read Grady's thoughts anymore."

Lucy put on a pair of gloves before wiping Alida's arm. "Interesting. Since most of the time, it's the opposite. After Kai and I mated, I could hear his thoughts and vice versa."

"Mated?" Grady asked. He needed a damn notepad to keep up with all the things they kept going over. But "mated" had come up a couple times, and Alida acted like it was nothing. From the worried look in Lucy's eyes, he wanted to know what it actually meant.

"It's kind of magical," Lucy said before pressing the needle into Alida's arm. "Shifters and supernatural people have one person made for them. Kai knew the second we were together that I was his mate. Most shifters feel it right away. There is this pull to be with the person. Even humans can feel it sometimes."

That explained why for the past few months, he couldn't go to sleep without walking by Alida's room first. No matter how much he tried distancing himself, he had this nagging pull in the back of his mind to go to her and be near her.

"Are we mates?" Grady asked Alida, even though he knew the answer.

She nodded. "It's hard to explain, but can we talk about it when we aren't around my family?" Her cheeks turned red, and Grady couldn't wait to figure out what crossed through her mind.

He was staring at Alida when he felt the prick in his arm. "Damn, don't you warn people before sticking a needle in them?"

Lucy shrugged and took a couple vials of his blood. She turned and went to the computers and started working.

"How long before we figure out what differs from my DNA?"

She placed it in a machine and turned back to him. "It shouldn't take long. Have you ever experienced something like this before?"

"Reading minds?" he asked.

"Yes."

"Nope. Until the other night, I thought everything I saw on TV was fiction. Now I'm not even sure what fiction is anymore. The next thing you guys are going to tell me is vampires are real, and you've met the devil."

The room became deathly quiet, and nobody would look him in the eye. "Are vampires a thing?"

Alida eyed him for a second before nodding. "They've become very civilized over the years. Well, that's what Dad tells me. He said over two hundred years ago, they used to eat whoever they wanted. Now they have a system, but I don't know much about it besides knowing that they don't take people's blood without asking. The council employs a few in case a human catches someone shifting. They can send a vampire to erase the human's memories."

Grady wasn't sure how he felt about vampires erasing people's memories. "I was worried for a second that you guys have met the devil."

Lucy shook her head. "I don't think any of us have met Lucifer. But we've met his daughter and son-in-law. They are really friendly people. Pandora told me the other day that Lucifer's bodyguard is a Pandacorn."

"Wait…The devil is real?" Grady asked.

Alida grabbed his hand. "We have a long time to figure everything out. You won't learn everything overnight. It will take time."

The computer made a beeping noise, and Lucy staredat the results. "Well, that can't be right."

Not the words he wanted to hear when someone was researching his DNA. For a doctor, she wasn't the best with bedside manners. But he also wasn't going to point that out since her husband was a dragon.

"What's not right?"

She stared at him, tilting her head as if he was a giant puzzle. "You have no shifter or supernatural DNA...You're human."

"Umm, I thought we already knew I was human."

Lucy placed his blood back on the machine and pushed a few more buttons. "It might take me a little longer to figure this out."

Alida grabbed his hand. "Let's go see if Uncle Kai figured out who is after me. Aunt Lucy isn't going to be much fun to talk to right now. Especially when she's found a puzzle."

The little scientist didn't even pay attention to them as they left the room and walked down the hall a few steps before walking into Kai's area. The lights were off. His computer screens illuminated the room. He had six large screens on the wall and a seventy-inch TV on the opposite wall in front of a couch.

"Did you find them?"

"Yes," he growled. "They were part of that same cult that killed themselves. Your roommate took pictures of you the day you moved in. She showed them to the people in the cult. Everyone was convinced you looked like the girl from the movie."

Grady thought back to the end of the movie when it flashed to when the girl was older. And the actress had looked a little like Alida. But he'd never put everything together, because it was just supposed to be a movie.

"But everyone died," Alida said.

Kai shook his head. "Not everyone in the cult. The

leader and a few of his close followers lived. They were coming after you. Boris was able to apprehend them. They are in custody. Nothing more for you to worry about. He was a longtime follower of Kael, and after the movie release, he got a following." Kai ran a hand over his face. "As for your mom, Grady, I can't seem to find her."

Grady hoped that meant she was no longer going to bother him. But he knew that wasn't the case. Something terrible was going to happen soon.

15

ALIDA

"*I*'m not watching that movie again!"

Hands on her hips, Alida stood in the living room next to her main bedroom. The entire wing of the house was quiet. After they got back from ice skating, they'd had hot chocolate with her family before going to their quiet spaces.

While she changed into one of Grady's shirts and shorts, he worked to find them a movie to watch.

"But it's like getting a glimpse into your childhood," he said with a smile spread across his face, but her eyes were distracted by his sexy abs. Over the past two weeks, she'd learned really fast why Grady looked so good. The guys were in her parents' home gym every day for two hours.

"You said the girl was unbelievable."

He winced. "Well, she grew up to be an unbelievably sexy woman that I can't keep my hands off," he told her. "Why don't you come over here and help me find something?"

Alida walked across the room, and Grady pulled her into his arms and pressed his lips to hers. They tasted like chocolate. She swiped her tongue across his lips again and moaned.

Grady pulled back too soon. "No sex in your parents' house," he whispered across her lips.

Nope, she was done with that rule, which Grady had made up on his own. Their relationship was moving forward in every way except the intimate one. Dammit, she wanted to mate with him, and he kept putting her off. Alida had explained everything to Grady about mating. But they hadn't talked about it again. Maybe he didn't want to be with her. Just the thought made a tear form in her eye. She'd never cried much before, but her emotions seemed to be different around Grady.

He leaned forward and kissed away the tear. "Hey? What's wrong?"

God, this guy knows how to make a woman melt in his arms.

Grady pulled back, slipped an arm around her, and led her to the couch. *Dammit.* She was going to have to talk about her feelings. Deep down, she worried he didn't want to be part of the supernatural world or be with someone like her.

"You never said if you wanted to, mate. And you keep not wanting…" She motioned to her body.

"Alida, look at me," he whispered, his fingers pressed below her chin so she would look up. "There is no question in my mind that I want to mate with you. As for not wanting to have sex—babe, I've been hard every second of the day. I want nothing more than to sink into you."

She glanced down at his athletic shorts. "Ohh," she whispered.

"But I don't want to disrespect your parents," he added, totally deflating her.

Alida would give him a little more time. Her parents had built her a house years ago on their land. But she liked being at home. Maybe it was time for her and Grady to spend time in their place. "Fine. But I don't want to watch that movie again. Parts of it are hard for me to watch."

"Do you miss your parents?" he whispered when she paused for too long.

"At times." Alida sighed. "But I never want Talia or Kirin to think it's because of them. They've given me a great life, but at times, I miss them. Even after I found out they made me in a test tube. Those early memories are fading a little, and I wonder if there will be a time that I don't even remember much about them. Can I ask you something?"

Grady nodded.

"Was your mother always a bitch?"

"Yes, there wasn't a time in my life that I remember her being a caring mother. The only time food was in the house was if child protective services was doing a visit. A few of the regular Joes would feel sorry for me and bring me food."

"Is that what made you want to go into psychology? To figure out why your mom was like the way she was?"

"No. When I was in foster care, I was angry at the world. Why did I have to have such a shitty mother when nobody else did? One of the last foster families I stayed with had me see a psychologist. And my outlook changed. I want to do that for others."

For weeks, Alida had watched Grady teach class. He took the extra step to ensure everyone understood what they needed to when working on the assignments. She knew he would do everything in his power to make sure his patients had the best care possible.

"Do you want kids?" he asked.

The question threw her for a second. Alida loved her brother, sister, and cousins. She wanted a large family one day. In the back of her mind, she worried about the genes she might pass on. "Yes, but not for a long time. I want to enjoy my life before I settle down and have kids." She smiled up at him. "Do you?"

"Before I met you, the answer would've been no. But so much changed in a short period, and I couldn't imagine the world without your children in it. I do agree that I'm not ready for kids either."

When he mentioned wanting kids, her heart leaped with joy. *But does he want to live in West Virginia?* The question was on the tip of her tongue, but she wasn't ready to talk about where they might live. She knew they had to head back to school in January. Grady only had one semester left.

Alida rested her head on Grady's bare chest as he flipped through the channels. "My parents built me a small house. There's no furniture in it."

"Why don't you stay there?"

"I like being around my family. Never needed privacy until I met you."

"Maybe we can check it out tomorrow," Grady hinted, his voice dropping. "I'm sure we would need to christen it before moving any furniture in."

Alida twined her fingers with his. "Do you think you would ever want to live in West Virginia?" She held her breath, waiting for his answer.

"My goal for the past few years was my education and a good job. I'm not sure if I will be able to get a job around here."

"The council would hire you in a heartbeat. Shifters always need…"

"I'll talk to your dad."

She shifted against Grady, and he groaned. "You know I could have us to the house within seconds."

The smile he sent her was enough to decide for both of them. She clutched the blanket on the couch and Grady then transported them.

***Grady

He would never get used to Alida's transporting. At

least now he didn't feel like he was going to throw up each time. That was a vast improvement.

They'd landed in the middle of an empty room, and Grady looked around the large space. His idea about a small place was utterly different from Alida's. He'd pictured a tiny two-bedroom home. Nope, the living room alone was larger than the house he'd expected to see.

Off to the side was a kitchen with large windows that overlooked the valley. If he had to guess, the place was enchanted like her parents' main house.

He knew Alida had been nervous to ask if he would want to live in West Virginia. What his angel didn't know was that he would do anything to make her happy. And he'd seen her smile more in the last two weeks than he'd seen in the three months she was in college.

Alida grabbed his hand and dragged him through the house. He counted at least five bedrooms and seven baths. When they came to the master, she walked in and spun in a circle. On the far wall was an electric fireplace. She dropped the blanket she'd brought on the floor and pressed the button to start the fireplace.

"Are you too cold?"

Alida walked over and wrapped her arms around his waist. "A bit, especially since we're going to be naked soon."

"I like the way you think." He pulled her down onto

the blanket. "I think you and I have a different idea of what a small house looks like." He chuckled.

"Technically, you've seen my parents' house and Uncle Kai's house. It is smaller compared to there. Don't get me wrong; I would never want a house that big or Athena."

Grady still wasn't sure about the AI in Kai's house. They'd stayed over at Kai's house for a couple of days so Lucy could run more tests. He'd almost slipped and fallen in the shower when the AI asked if she could adjust the water temp. There were some places he just wanted to be left alone. The bathroom was one of those places.

"I think we can both agree that our home will never have AI. I don't care how much your uncle coded the technology. Some things should never exist."

"It's nice how we agree on so many things."

"I think I'm falling in love with you," Alida said.

"Good, because I know I'm already in love with you, Alida. I can't imagine my life with anyone else."

"I might get more powers," she said with a bit of a warning.

"And we will deal with everything that comes at us," he said before pressing his lips to hers.

***Alida*

"I love my parents' house, but this feels so much better." Alida curled up on the blanket next to the fireplace.

"Yes, now I don't have to worry about your little

brother running in on us. Don't get me wrong. I like spending time with him." Grady placed a kiss on her collarbone. "So what do we have to do to mate?"

She hadn't expected the question. "During sex, I bind my powers to you."

"You won't blow the place up, will you?"

"My dad's been telling you too many stories." She was ninety percent sure she wouldn't kill them. Last time they were together, her powers had come out and wanted to bind to Grady.

"I'm ready if you are." He slid his hand down her side and cupped her ass.

Being near Grady was intoxicating, and it made it hard to think. But she knew more than anything he was her one true mate. "Me too."

"Good, because I've been hard for the past two weeks. Sleeping next to you in bed has given me permanent blue balls." He ran his fingers along the waistband of her shorts and slowly pulled them down.

Alida wanted nothing more than to connect her soul with Grady's. "I need you, Grady."

His pupils dilated, and she knew he needed her as much as she needed him. She pulled the shirt over her head, and Grady reached around and unhooked her bra. He captured her nipple between his lips. His lips alone on her skin was almost enough to make her go over the edge.

Grady quickly discarded his clothes and nudged her legs apart before he slowly pulled her panties down, tracing his fingers along her legs. "I love how your eyes turn purple when you're turned on," he whispered against her skin before he captured her clit between his lips.

"Grady, you make the world disappear."

He pressed a finger inside her, and her body arched off the blanket, pressing her clit against his mouth. She was gasping with each stroke of his hand.

"I need more," she begged. When he reached up and pinched her nipple, it sent her over the edge. She screamed his name. "Please."

Grady pressed himself into her, and her magic shrouded them in a bubble. Nothing could get to them. Pink and purple swirled around as he worked himself in and out.

They were both so close to the edge, she let her magic take over, and it wrapped them both in a warm blanket. Grady pressed his thumb to her clit. The slight touch was enough to make her wild and go over the edge, but this time, Grady went with her. She felt a sense of peace wash over her.

"I love you," she whispered as he pulled her in tight.

16

GRADY

*G*rady couldn't believe how much his vision of the world had changed in the last week. Alida and her family had explained how the supernatural world worked. He'd even gotten to the point where he didn't throw up when Alida transported him.

The council had replaced his car with a brand-new BMW. He'd tried to decline, but Alida's dad didn't seem to take no for an answer. Christmas Eve was only a few days away. The gift he'd bought for Alida was in his car, which was in pieces. He planned to get her a new one today. Grady let out a sigh, knowing the threat against Alida was gone for now. He took that as a huge win.

His mother had contacted him once, letting him know there was a slight delay. Lucy was still trying to figure out the lineage of his DNA. She was running it across all the databases, but it kept coming up blank. She couldn't even find anyone with matching DNA in the human system. She'd joked a couple of times that he might be an alien. *God, I hope that's not the case.*

The group after Alida was part of the same cult that Alida's roommate had belonged to. But after her uncle did further research, they'd figured out the cult was part of a group really trying to bring Kael back to life. Kirin had made a call to the shifter king Antonio, and he'd promised Kael was right where he belonged in the afterlife.

Grady wanted more answers than a promise. *How sure could this guy be that Kael was dead?*

Kirin told Grady he trusted Antonio, and if anyone one knew, it would be him. With how much he still needed to learn about the supernatural world, he wondered what else was out there. Grady shook his head. Sometimes, he thought about things until his head hurt. He had a feeling Kirin was going to offer him a job today, but he wasn't sure how Alida felt about it. They'd talked before about him working for the council, but he wanted her to be happy about it. She seemed calm and more carefree in West Virginia. All he wanted was for her to be happy.

She was nothing like his mother. For years, Grady had never wanted a family or kids, because he pictured his mother every time he pictured his future. It was strange how one person could change his entire outlook on the future.

When they'd mated, peace had washed over him. He was also relieved when he didn't get any more-extreme magical powers. His strength increased, and when he'd cut his finger slicing onions, the cut had healed faster, but he didn't have the powers to transport, move items, or blow things up. Grady was happy with mind-reading, mostly since he'd learned to turn it off.

Grady sensed her walking into the bedroom. He hadn't made his mind up for which dress shirt he planned to wear today. He was around her family every day, but he still wanted to impress her dad.

"You sure you don't want me to come with you?" Alida paused. "My dad can be very persuasive."

He had no doubt her dad would work to convince him. He also needed to prove himself to her father. "I can handle your dad," Grady said, pulling her into his arms. "What we need to figure out is what we want. Because no matter what your dad threatens me with or promises, I'm not deciding about our future without your input."

Our future. He'd thought he already had that planned out.

"He's going to want you to work for the council."

"Does that bother you?"

"No. We already talked about it." She rested her head on his chest. "But I don't want you to change your future because of me. We could figure out a way to make both of our dreams come true. Were mated now."

"And what is your dream, Alida?"

He would do anything to make it happen.

"To take over for my dad one day," she whispered.

He sat down on the bed and pulled her onto his lap. She was already in danger because of her powers. Sitting at the head of the West Virginia council would make her an even bigger target. But he also knew that she would do an outstanding job leading everyone.

"So you want your dad's job. You want me to negotiate that today also," he joked. "I'm serious when I say I won't take anything without talking to you first. Yes, you want to take over the council one day, but do you want to head back to DC and finish school there, or do you want to finish online? I looked online. My remaining classes, I can take online, but I spent years in college getting to go to frat parties and making friends."

"It was hard for me to make friends at college."

Alida hadn't gone out to party like everyone else. He watched her for months as she read in the common area or binge watched TV. Grady liked that he could see her each night and didn't have to worry about something terrible happening at a frat party.

"Many of your friends are in Florida. Would you rather move there?"

The first time he'd heard her on the phone with Carl, a wave of jealousy had overtaken him. But then he'd talked to the man, and they'd since become good friends. He couldn't wait to meet him after New Year's.

"We can always transport to Florida, but West Virginia is where my family is. And we have a house, even though it's empty. Are you sure you would be okay with not finishing your degree in DC?"

"Yes." There was no hesitation in his voice. "Even if we stay here, that doesn't mean I'm always going to work for the council. Once I get my degree, I would love to open my own practice."

"I support anything you want."

"I thought you would always want me to work for the council." He wasn't sure what Kirin was going to offer him.

"Enough talking about my father. Kiss me."

"You don't have to tell me twice." His lip twitched before he leaned forward and pressed a kiss to her soft cherry lips.

His tongue slipped past her lips, and she tightened her arms around his neck. She pressed her hips forward, causing him to groan. Unfortunately, Kara, Alida's younger sister, stomped into the room, "Gross."

Alida pulled back and rested her head against his chest. "What do you need, Kara?"

"Sis, are you going to help decorate the gingerbread houses?" Kara asked.

Alida had told him the gingerbread houses were a Christmas tradition. A few days before Christmas Eve, she and her siblings would decorate cookies and gingerbread houses. He wanted to give her time with her siblings, so he'd put off taking the meeting with Alida's dad until today. He also needed to get her Christmas present.

Alida pulled out of his arms and stood up. He immediately missed the touch of her skin.

"Yes, save me the one with the crack on the side. I have an idea. Just give me a few minutes, and I'll be down."

"Five minutes, and if you're not down, I'm going to decorate both houses." She turned and stormed out of the room. Alida's sister had a little bit of an attitude.

Alida's lip twitched, and she disappeared for a second before reappearing, holding the gingerbread house in question. She set it to the side before sitting back down on the bed next to him.

He heard Kara scream, "Not fair" from down the hall.

"Are you sure you're okay with me taking a job here, and we could go back for my last semester?"

Alida nodded. "I had this pull that made me want to go to DC for school. I'm not sure there was anything that could've stopped me. It's gone. I don't even care about going back next semester. As long as I'm with you, that's all that matters. I love you, Grady."

He loved hearing those words out of her mouth. She was the first person to ever say them to him. His mother had never uttered the words once.

"Did I say something wrong?"

"No. I love you more. You know we're going to have to save for furniture. I'm not sure how long I can live with your family. Especially since I want to see you naked and pregnant." The words slipped out of his mouth. He hadn't planned on saying them. It was early. Yes, he wanted kids, but down the road.

"I like that. As for the furniture, I overheard Mom talking about getting someone to decorate the place. I wouldn't be surprised if that isn't our Christmas present. As for kids, I want to wait until we've had enough time together."

"Yes, I agree, not for a while." He leaned in and pressed a kiss to her lips. "I know we are figuring out a lot fast. I just want to be on the same page."

His phone beeped, reminding him it was time to go. "Have fun with your siblings."

"Good luck."

Alida walked him to his new car and kissed him before he got in. Grady put his new phone in the center console. The council had replaced that, along with a wardrobe. He wasn't sure how it happened, but the next day, clothes in the perfect size had shown up. His phone even had all of his contacts and messages. He assumed Alida's uncle Kai had done that.

Grady hadn't gone to the council building yet. He put the address into the navigation system and turned out of the driveway. He still wasn't used to the optical illusions that hid Alida's parents' house. It was strange driving straight through a brick wall. Grady sighed when he was on the other side of the barrier.

He followed the Australian-accented navigation system as she told him to take a right turn. Ten minutes later, he pulled into a gravel parking lot and stared at a large building that looked like a warehouse. He spotted the cameras on the corners, filming everything, and the sizeable seven-foot guard at the door was an indicator he was at the right place.

Grady walked up to the guard. With each step, the guy seemed larger. Without saying anything, the guard opened the door and grunted. Grady walked through the door and stepped up to the desk. A small blond woman sat behind it. Her desk was lined with snow globes. It almost seemed like glitter was falling from the ceiling.

She smiled up at him. "Oh, you're Alida's mate. I'm Oliva." As if on cue, she threw a handful of glitter into the air.

Grady tried to step back, but he wasn't fast enough. His black suit was now covered in pink and gold glitter. "I'm here to see Kirin," Grady gritted out, trying not to yell at the woman.

"His office is at the end of the hall. Have a great day." She reached for another handful of glitter, but he got out of the way more quickly that time.

Kirin sat behind a large oak desk, a scowl across his face. Grady worked to keep his powers locked in a box. He didn't want to know what the dragon was thinking.

An hour later, they agreed to him taking a job at the council. He was the counselor everyone could talk to. He was excited and nervous to start at the council. Over the next few months, he would work part-time while finishing his degree online. He no longer needed to TA or take care of the dorms to pay for his college. The council would pay for it. Grady wondered if it was Kirin who was paying.

When he left the building, he dodged the front desk, went out to his car, and called Alida.

"Hello. Was Dad nice?"

"I got the job!"

"Did you think you wouldn't? Are you on your way home now?"

"I have to make one stop, and then I will be."

"Can you grab us some more chocolate chips? Kyle ate them all."

"Sure, I'll see you in an hour."

"Love you."

"Love you too." Grady pressed the end button on his steering wheel.

He couldn't wait to start his new job after the holidays. He and Alida planned to spend a few days in Florida. Then they would need to move into their new house. Everything in his life was going so well. Worry set in a little. Nothing had ever been this easy for him.

Grady pulled into the mall parking lot. He cut the engine, grabbed his phone, and got out of the car. When he was halfway across the parking lot, his phone rang, and he looked down and sighed. Things had been going too well. He didn't need to see a number to know it was his mom.

He swiped across the screen. "What do you want?"

"Run."

He didn't have time to ask a follow-up question. A hand wrapped around his face seconds before a white van stopped in front of him. He struggled against the arm as the person placed a cloth over his nose.

He never made it home to celebrate with Alida. He worried about what would happen to her now that they were mated. He hoped she would find someone else—that was his last thought before everything went black.

17

ALIDA

"*H*e's not answering his phone," Alida said as she paced back and forth in the kitchen. She stopped for a second to check the time on her phone for the millionth time.

"Maybe the mall is busy, or he's struggling to find you a present," her mother said, but the worry in Talia's eyes told a different story.

Grady would've answered one of her texts if he were still shopping, even if he was only thirty minutes late. Her gut twisted, and she knew that instant that something was wrong. Her mom stopped her from teleporting to the mall. Alida knew it would be dangerous, but every cell in her body screamed something wasn't right. Kai and Lucy were still working on figuring out who Grady's dad was. She hoped he hadn't gone to meet his mother alone.

Her phone dinged, and she glanced down to see a

text from her dad, letting her know he was on his way home. She glanced out the window as a fresh coat of snow came down. He could've lost control on the road. Or maybe the supernatural life was too much for him, and he'd decided to head back to DC. She couldn't stop the bad thoughts from rushing through her head.

She closed her eyes for a second. The last thought didn't even make sense since he'd met with her dad before heading to the mall. Maybe someone was still after her, and they were going to use Grady to get to her.

"We will find him," Talia said, wrapping her in a motherly hug.

Alida couldn't help letting the tear finally fall. Her mother had admitted things weren't right. The second her dad got to the house, she planned on going to Uncle Kai's and making him figure out where Grady's car was. Her every instinct told her someone had taken him, but she didn't know who would actually find him in West Virginia.

"What happens if we're too late?" she asked, pulling away from her mother and sitting down on the chair. The excitement from cooking with her family had faded away. The gingerbread house and turtles she'd made with her siblings instead of going with Grady sat on the counter. He'd told her he loved turtles, and she'd made them just for him.

"Here." Talia handed her a Kleenex. "Grady is smart.

He'll figure out a way to help us find him. I also have all the faith in Kirin."

As if just saying his name conjured up her dad, he came storming into the house. His eyes were bright orange. "Let's go," he growled.

She didn't need to be asked twice. Alida grabbed onto both of her parents, and a second later, they were in Kai's computer lab. Her uncle didn't even flinch as they appeared next to him.

His fingers were flying across the keyboard. On the screen was the camera feed from the mall parking lot. Grady's car was parked three spots from the front door. She watched closely as Kai rewound the footage of Grady pulling into the parking lot.

Her eyes didn't leave the monitor as he walked across the street, stopped, pulled out his phone, and placed it to his ear. He glanced around the lot before the monitor flashed black for a second. When the feed came back, Grady wasn't standing in the street any longer.

What the fuck?

Kai rewound and replayed the footage. The same thing happened. On the other screen, footage inside the mall played, but Grady never walked in. She knew something bad happened in those seconds leading up to him disappearing.

Alida pulled out her phone and called Grady again. Now it was going straight to voicemail. Before, it had at least rang a few times.

Her anger caused the air in the room to become thick. Kai glared at her for a second, but she couldn't tamp down her magic. For a second, she thought about reminding them how they'd acted when they almost lost their mates. At the time, she'd seen the future and known everything would be okay. But she couldn't see her own future.

"Can you track his phone?" Alida asked.

"Already did. Its last location was the parking lot. If you look closely on the camera, you can see it on the ground."

Alida stepped forward, squinted, and saw the phone crushed to pieces on the ground. "What about the last call he received?"

"The number was blocked. I'm working on hacking the telephone company to trace the number." Kai ran his hands through his hair. "It would be easier if you all stepped back for a second."

Her parents went over to the couch in the living room and sat down next to her brother and sister. There was no way she would leave Kai's side until he came up with the intel she wanted.

"We need to hurry. I know he's alive, but something is off."

Kai glanced at her. "Normally, feelings like that only happen after mating."

She glanced toward the couch, and her father was on his feet, stomping across the room. He stopped next to her and glared.

"You guys, mated." It came out more like a statement. "I'm not sure if I care if we find him anymore. You're too young to mate. Maybe ten more years, yes. Hell, if I would have known, no way would I have offered him a job."

"I'm twenty-two years old, Dad. You know he was my mate. But this is very weird to talk about with you."

"But you're my baby girl."

She couldn't help but roll her eyes. "And he's my mate."

Kai turned and looked at her. "I understand, but I need some time. Go see if Lucy has any new information for us."

Alida watched the screens for a second before she turned and walked out of Kai's computer room and down the hall to the lab. She heard her mom's footsteps behind her.

The door to the state-of-the-art lab was open. As she walked through the door, Alida could hear Lucy talking to herself. Her aunt was staring at her computer screens like it was a giant puzzle she was trying to figure out. Her younger cousin was next to Lucy, wearing a matching lab coat, mimicking Lucy's gesture. She stopped and smiled for a second before walking up behind Lucy.

Alida didn't understand any of the information on the screens. At least when she looked at Kai's, it was video footage. Lucy's was numbers and other data she couldn't make sense of.

"Find anything?" Alida asked, hoping for some break.

"Nothing," Lucy said.

Lucy searched the prison database for Grady's mom's DNA, but it was gone, along with any evidence she was ever in prison. Grady's foster records were also gone from the system.

"FOUR HOURS." Alida sighed as she sat down in the chair next to Kai. "Wait, who is that?"

An image of an older man having lunch at a café across from the man who was tailing Grady for the last few months was on the screen.

"Dr. Yeager," he barked back. "He's a neurosurgeon at the hospital in DC. The guy in the chair next to him is his son. I couldn't find a link back to Grady."

Fuck. She recognized him, but he'd aged a lot over the years. "There was a picture of him with my dad. It was before I was born."

"Are you sure?"

Before leaving home, Alida had digitized all of her photos. She pulled up the link and scrolled back until she found the photo.

"They look alike," Talia mumbled. "Also, notice how his son looks like Grady?"

"We know Alida's dad worked with many scientists

to come up with the perfect shifter." Her uncle winced, knowing the words sounded clinical.

Alida had come to terms with her progeny years ago. She also didn't hold her dad's scientific experiments against him, especially when he'd destroyed the research to protect her. "What if I wasn't the first test case? Maybe my dad worked with other scientists."

"You think Grady was part of an experiment?" Kai pulled up old photos of Dr. Yeager. "He is a neurosurgeon. Besides the one photo you have of him and your father together, I can't find anything. We always assumed he used another shifters' DNA for the mindreading. What would they want with Grady now?"

"Do you think it's possible they knew I was his mate?" Alida asked, not sure how anyone would know before them. She worried for a second that something had messed with their DNA, making it so they would automatically be mates, but there was no saying she would decide that college except for the pull she had to go.

"I think it's not a coincidence. If you look at Grady's mother, she wasn't supposed to get out of jail ever. Her first year in prison, she killed someone."

Kai pulled up the logs of the visitors who had been to visit Grady's mom. She hadn't had one visitor in years, until a few weeks before the school year started. The day after the visit, they'd released her from prison. Kai pulled up the camera feed from the day she had the visitor.

"Right there…" Kirin stated as a man walked into the visitor room. His back was always to the camera, like he knew where each camera was located.

The ID he'd given at the check-in was fake and didn't give them any information. The guy also wore a hat covering his hair.

"She doesn't look happy," Kai pointed out.

Grady's mom was yelling at the person across from her. The man didn't seem to care, but they couldn't see or hear what he was saying. When he stood to leave, he pulled the hat down, covering his face so they could never see who it was. Grady's mom sat in her chair a second longer, glaring at the man as he walked away.

"Have you found Grady's mom?" Alida asked.

"No, she checked out of the hotel weeks ago. I have seen no sign of her since then. It's like she disappeared —or they got rid of her," Kai muttered.

"We need to narrow down locations of where he would take Grady. This is our only option," Kirin said.

Kai nodded and pulled up all the property Dr. Yeager owned. He had four places and one under a shell company. The one buried under unique identities was in the middle of nowhere—a perfect location to hide someone.

"Let's go," Alida said.

Kirin placed a hand on her shoulder. "I think you should stay here with your mom and aunt. Kai, Conley, and I will go."

For years, Alida let her dad and uncles go after the

bad guys. There was no way she would sit back and not go. "I'm going."

Her father's jaw ticked for a second before he nodded. She grabbed Kai and her dad before transporting to her uncle Conley's house. When they were all ready, she transported to the edge of the woods near the abandoned building.

She listened but couldn't hear a thing. They worked themselves around the side. The white van they'd seen in the satellite feed wasn't parked out front any longer. Alida prayed they weren't too late.

Kirin opened the side door. A few cuss words came out of his mouth before they stepped into the deserted building.

It was empty. Alida closed her eyes and was hit by the smell of blood. She knew without getting it tested that it was Grady's blood, and he was gone. They were too late.

18

GRADY

"I will not do it!" Grady growled. He tried to move his arm, but it didn't budge. His life was about to be over, and there was no way he would let the person who'd strapped him down get what he wanted.

His eyes wandered back to the clock on the wall. Five hours ago, his life had changed again. Meeting his dad—or his half-brother—for the first time hadn't gone the way he'd envisioned it as a kid. Even with his new strength after mating, he couldn't break the bonds around his wrists.

Alida and her family would have no way to trace his location. His kidnappers had thrown his phone out the window as they sped away.

"All you need to do is read the man's thoughts," Riken, his half-brother, growled.

Grady's eyes darted to his mother and the man they

said was his father. She had on the same red dress she'd worn the other day, but it was now stained with dirt, and her eye was black and blue. His dad didn't look much better—blood trickled down his forehead.

Grady read everyone's thoughts the second he woke up. His father was shocked to learn he had a son with Grady's mother. His mother had been part of an experiment. They'd paid her a hefty sum to carry a baby, whom she would turn over to them.

According to his dad, none of the embryos had survived. His mother had taken the money and kept the kid. Grady was part of the first experiment placing shifter genes in babies' DNA. But his power hadn't turned on until he'd formed the connection with Alida. Grady still denied he could hear anyone's thoughts.

His brother stomped across the warehouse and held a knife to his mother's neck. Grady wished he felt the need to save her life, but she'd been evil for so many years. And she could've given him up when he was born.

Riken wrapped his hands in his mother's hair and pressed a blade to her neck. "Tell me how I can turn on the same power. He has to know."

"I don't know what you're talking about." Grady struggled with the leather strap around his wrist. "I can't read his mind. That's the stupidest thing I've ever heard."

Riken narrowed his eyes and stepped to the side, placing the knife to Dr. Yaeger's neck. Technically, he was only a sperm donor, but Grady felt like he needed to save the man.

The drug Riken had used to knock him out was still having a slight effect on Grady. It was hard to concentrate, but he tried to listen to Riken's thoughts. He couldn't hear a thing. His brother was working to block him out.

A loud bang sounded from the side of the warehouse as a man in a leather jacket walked across the warehouse and stopped in front of Grady's mother. He held up the gun and pressed the trigger. His mother screamed for a couple of seconds before her bullet entered her chest.

"Grady, you have the choice to join us or end up like your worthless mother," the newcomer said.

"I don't even know who you are," Grady spat out, jerking his ties. "How do I know you won't kill me the second I give you what you want?" Grady couldn't read this guy's mind either. When he tried, it was black. But he also got a sickening feeling like the man was pure evil.

"Zack. I'm Dr. Yeager and Dr. Meadows', true fuck up. I might kill you, but if you want your precious girlfriend Alida to live, you will do as I say."

"She's not my girlfriend." His stomach clenched as he said the words. Grady would walk away from everything to protect her. He would also die, making sure nothing ever happened to Alida.

The first chance he had, he would kill this man for even thinking about hurting a hair on Alida's head.

"You were the first experiment Dr. Yeager and Dr. Meadows were able to make. I'm somewhere in the middle of the failed experiments, and Alida was the only one that truly came to what Dr. Meadows wanted. For you and me, they used drug addicts as a surrogate, but for Alida, they used Dr. Meadow's wife. The rest of us were thrown to the side. But it's time I make my own set of experiments. I just need the information out of his head." He tossed a knife between his hands.

Grady felt the leather loosening on his right hand. He also wondered how many more experiments were left out in the world. "If you think I can read minds and we're part of some grand experiment, why don't you read Dr. Yeager's thoughts? And it's not like he's thinking about the experiment this second. Not sure what you think I can pull out of his mind."

Grady mentally kicked himself for giving too much information.

"I knew you could read minds. For years, I watched his scientists' projects from afar. When I figured out Alida was going to college in DC, I hacked the system and put her on your floor. The experiments seem to tie to one another. We aren't the only ones, but we are the only ones left alive."

"You killed others?" Grady asked.

Grady watched as Zack's lips turned into the nastiest smile he'd ever seen.

"They served their purpose," he sneered. His eyes flashed red for a second. "Time to go. Get her in the van."

Zack nodded and dragged his mother out of the building. Grady needed to make a run for it, because staying with this crazed lunatic wasn't an option. He glanced back at his dad and read his thoughts. "He can't read minds, but he can sense people way before they arrive if he's moving us. Someone has found out where we are. I'm sorry this happened to you. I honestly didn't know so many existed."

"Why do you want to leave? I thought you wanted me to read his mind?" Grady asked. He was trying to think of a way to stall as much as possible. He worried the crazed man would go after Alida next. The strap on Grady's arm finally broke loose. He kept it in place, not wanting to show Zack he was almost free.

"This wasn't where I planned to take you, but your bitch of a mother made things difficult. Not sure why suddenly she wanted to save your life. Probably because she thought she could get more money for you once she figured out you had some type of powers." Zack glared. "Time to go back to where it all started."

The drive to DC would take at least five hours—plenty of time for him to come up with a plan to take Zack down. Grady's half-brother walked back into the warehouse. He looked nervous about Zack. Grady couldn't blame him. Grady wasn't quite sure how he knew it, but Zack felt like pure evil.

Riken uncuffed his father and pulled him to his feet. Dr. Yeager grunted as Riken shoved him toward the warehouse door.

Grady quickly unleashed his other hand while they weren't paying attention. But he wasn't fast enough. Zack swung around and punched him in the gut as he went to stand. The force knocked the wind out of him.

Grady stumbled back and barely had time to recover before the next below hit him in the jaw. He dropped to the ground and spat blood out on the floor. He took a couple of seconds, getting his bearings before he stood and squared off with Zack.

"You really think you can take me out?" Zack asked.

"Yes," Grady countered. Outside, Grady faintly heard the van start and pull away.

Zack's eyes widened for a second, and he turned toward the door. Grady used that second to punch him in the side. The large man dropped to the ground.

"I'm going to kill you!" he yelled as he slowly stood.

Grady didn't wait. He took off, running out the side door and into the woods. The cold snow crunched under his boots as he ran. The snow made it hard to cover up his tracks.

A gun fired behind him, and the bullet hit the tree next to him. But Grady kept running. To the side, he saw a flash, and three people appeared. Alida was here, and now she would be in danger. Grady kept running in the opposite direction, hoping Zack hadn't noticed them appear.

He stopped paying attention to what was in front of him and tripped over a large rock. Pain radiated through his chin as he fell to the ground. Zack must have been a lot faster than him—when Grady went to stand, a foot connected with his side sending him back to the ground. Grady's mouth was still bleeding from the cut. Blood dripped into the snow as he huffed, trying to catch his breath. He still couldn't read the man's thoughts, only darkness.

"If you kill me, you won't get what you want."

The man sneered down at him, "You aren't worth the trouble. I can find Dr. Yeager again and torture the information out of him. It will be nice seeing the supernatural princess crying over you. Might just be worth it setting my project on hold."

Zack extended his arm, pointing a gun straight at Grady. He watched as the man's finger squeezed around the trigger. But in a blink of an eye, a flash appeared next to him, and he disappeared back to the warehouse. Grady landed on the hard floor of the warehouse, hunched over, and puked. His head spun from the quick transport.

"Are you okay?" Alida asked as she knelt next to him. "I didn't mean to make you sick. It was a split-second decision."

And it had probably saved his life. But he needed to get back up and go after Zack. That man needed to pay for killing those people, even if his mother had turned him over so she could make a quick dollar. "We need to go after him."

Grady stood, but he needed to hold on to the chair as his world spun around him. He took a wobbly step toward the door but let out a sigh as Alida's dad walked in with Zack in handcuffs. Grady sighed and slumped down in the chair. "My half-brother took off with my sperm donor dad. And he killed my mom. I think she's in the van with them."

Kirin tapped his ear. "Your mom isn't dead. Lots of blood loss. We will take her to the council to heal. As for your half-brother, he didn't think this guy was going to be so crazy, so he took off with his dad. It was all a stint for him to pay more attention. Conley is on his way back with the van. We're going to take them all in. Why don't you guys head back to the house? I know your mom wants to see you."

He wanted to protest and go help take everyone into jail. But the fight, along with the drugs, made it hard for him to function.

"Let's go home," Alida said before wrapping her arms around him. Grady closed his eyes as they transported to her bedroom. When he knew it was coming, he wasn't as sick.

Alida pressed her forehead to his. "Don't ever get kidnapped again. I knew the moment something was wrong. My blood felt like it was on fire, and you wouldn't answer your phone."

He slid his hand to her lower back and dragged his

fingers along the bottom of her shirt. His other hand cupped her face as he touched his lips to hers. The kiss wasn't gentle. It was full of need, proof they were both okay. His tongue pushed past her lips and explored her mouth.

Alida moaned as she pushed her breasts against his chest. At that moment, he knew he would do everything in his power to always get back to her. No crazy sibling or relative was going to stop him. Alida was his mate. His other half. The only person to make him feel complete.

He walked her backward until they hit the bed. In a quick movement, he broke the kiss and swooped her up into his arms before putting her in the center. His lips were back against her as she moaned from each swipe of his tongue.

Grady pulled back and rested his forehead against hers. "I love you, Alida."

"I love you too." She pulled him down into a kiss.

"Good morning, beautiful," Grady said, rolling over in the bed and pulling Alida into his arms.

They'd stayed in their new house for the past two days, but today, they would need to go to Alida's parents' house for Christmas dinner. It was their first Christmas together, and he couldn't imagine waking up any other way than with Alida tucked into his arms.

Two days ago, he'd thought he would never see her again. Even with all the danger in the supernatural world, he wouldn't give it up for anything as long as he had Alida by his side. He planned on taking fighting classes at the council to help protect his family.

Her light-gray eyes flickered open. They'd spent the previous day in bed, and Grady really wanted to spend another day with her legs wrapped around him.

Life was perfect. Every time they were together, their bond intensified. Grady could now sense her mood. He was still happy he couldn't hear her thoughts. It let him rest his mind around her. He was just grateful to have the woman he loved in his arms.

Grady's father was coming to dinner, and he wasn't completely sure how he felt about it or what the man had done many years ago. But Dr. Yaeger was now working with Kirin to make sure there weren't any other children left alone. Meanwhile, Grady's mother was back in prison, where she belonged. She'd asked to see him before they sent her away, but he decided she wasn't worth his time.

He was done looking into the past. The only thing that mattered was their future.

"I love how quiet our new house is," Alida said as she ran her fingers over his naked skin.

Her touch alone sent his body on fire. Damn, he was a lucky man.

He'd found a tough, strong, and smart woman. Grady planned to never let her get away.

"I'm still in shock it was completely decorated."

When Kirin had gotten back to the house after taking everyone to the council, he and Talia had handed them the keys and told them to go stay in their house and not come back until Christmas day. No one needed to tell them twice. Alida had transported them straight to their new home, which even had a Christmas tree in the living room.

"I think my mom can read the future sometimes. Let's go make breakfast and open our gifts." Alida rolled out of bed and let the sheet drop from her body.

He stared at her ass as she walked to the dresser and threw on his white T-shirt from the day before. The shirt engulfed her, but he loved seeing her wear his clothing.

Grady grabbed his gym shorts and threw them on then found Alida in the living room, holding two gifts —one he bought and one she bought. They had to run back to the mall so he could get her something since the kidnapping had cut his original trip short.

They curled up on the couch together. A fire flickered in the fireplace, and snow fell outside. They couldn't have asked for a more perfect Christmas.

Grady was nervous about the gift he'd bought for Alida. He hadn't planned on getting her a ring yet. But the council had put a huge sign-on bonus into his account. He figured it was more from her dad than anything, so he'd used the money so they could start their future.

"I'm going to open mine first," Grady said, taking the small box from her hands and peeling it open. Inside was a nice watch.

Alida stared up at him, biting her lip. "Losing you the other day almost killed me. This watch doesn't only tell time, but...it has a tracker. Saying it out loud sounds creepy and not a good gift. But I can't lose you again."

Grady tugged at her blond curl until she looked him

in the eye. "It's not a creepy gift at all. I promise to wear it every day. As long as I can get a tracker for you too."

She smiled at him and pulled the diamond necklace away from her skin. "I have one. Uncle Kai tracks us all. Not in a creepy way, but to make sure we're safe."

He leaned forward and pressed his lips to hers. "Thank you." He got up and knelt in front of the couch. "Alida—"

"Yes!" she cut him off.

"You don't want me to ask?" he joked.

"You don't need to. The answer is yes."

She cupped both of his cheeks and pressed her lips to his. Grady pulled back and pushed the diamond ring onto her finger. Her eyes sparkled with tears as he picked her up and carried her back to bed. They were going to be late for their first Christmas.

Five years later – Christmas morning - Alida

Alida stared down at her ring. Grady had given it to her five years ago. The ring still sparkled in the light. So much had changed over the years. Grady had finished his doctorate and opened his own practice in town. Alida had taken her place at her father's side on the council. She loved working with him.

She didn't need to turn to know her mom was standing next to her as she stared out into the back yard, watching the kids build a snowman. Her brother and sister stood to the side while the cousins built.

"Are you going to tell the family today?" Talia asked.

There was no point in playing dumb to her mother's question. She hadn't planned on telling the family yet. Tonight, she was going to tell Grady. "I didn't plan on it. How long have you known?"

Her mother gave her a pointed look. "For a while. Your dad knows too, dear. Why haven't you told Grady yet? I know that man worships the ground you walk on."

He did, and she wanted to tell him, but he'd been so busy with the practice. She didn't want him to worry. Alida had gone to the doctor because of bad cramps, and her doctor had told her to take it easy. If she told Grady, he would stop everything and make sure she was okay.

As if hearing his name, he walked over and wrapped his arms around her, resting his hands on her stomach.

Alida grabbed Grady's hand and led him through the house to the balcony off the side. When they walked outside, she placed a bubble around them, making it so it was warm. Over the past few years, she'd perfected her magic, and there were a lot fewer mishaps.

Grady sat on one chair and pulled her into his lap. "You are finally going to tell me you're pregnant."

"How long have you known?" she asked.

His hands brushed across her breasts, and she

couldn't help but moan. "A while. Why haven't you wanted to tell me?"

"At first, I had complications," she whispered.

Grady wrapped his arms around her tighter.

She didn't want to worry him, and everything was clear now. "I'm fine now, and our little boy is doing great."

"Boy?" he asked, running his hands over her belly.

"Yes, in six months, we're going to be parents."

"Have I told you how much I love you?"

"Ten times a day," she laughed.

"I don't care what brought us together. I couldn't be happier, and I can't wait to meet this little guy."

Alida was excited about the next chapter of their lives.

The end.

BANISHED WOLF is now available.

CLICK HERE to get your copy so that you can keep reading this series today!

You can join my newsletter for update release information. CLICK HERE!

OTHER TITLES BY LILY WINTER

Fated Mates of the Underworld
Banished Wolf
Claimed Witch
Exiled Demigod
Immortal Dragon
The Dragon's Psychic
The Dragon's Human
The Dragon's Mate
The Dragon's Hunt
The Dragon's Wolf
The Dragon's Prophecy

ROMANTIC SUSPENSE BOOKS BY LINZI BAXTER

Lily's alter ego

White Hat Security Series
Hacker reExposed
Royal Hacker
Misunderstood Hacker
Undercover Hacker
Hacker Revelation
Hacker Christmas
Hacker Salvation
Hacker Enclosed
Hacker Wedding - Jan 12, 2021
Nova Satellite Security Series
(White Hat Security Spin Off)

Pursuing Phoenix

Pursuing Aries

Pursuing Pegasus

Pursuing Columbia Mar 30, 2021

Pursuing Cygnus May 25, 2021

A Flipping Love Story (Special Forces World)

Unlocking Dreams

Unlocking Hope

Unlocking Love

Unlocking Desire

Unlocking Secrets Apr 27, 2021

Unlocking Lies

Montana Gold (Brotherhood Protector World)

Grayson's Angel

Noah's Love

Bryson's Treasure

Visit linzibaxter.com for more information and release dates.

Join Linzi Baxter Newsletter at Newsletter

ABOUT AUTHOR

Lily Winter lives in Orlando, Florida with her husband and lazy basset hound. She started writing when voices inside her head wouldn't stop talking until the story was told. When not at work as an IT Manager, Lily enjoys writing action-packed paranormal romances that will take you to the edge of your seat.

She enjoys engaging her readers with strong, interesting characters that have complex and stimulating stories to tell. If you enjoy a little (or maybe a whole lot) of steam and spice, don't miss checking out White Hat Security series.

When not writing, Lily enjoys reading, watching college sports (GO UCF Knights), and traveling to Europe. She loves hearing from her readers and can't wait to hear from you!

Made in the USA
Las Vegas, NV
11 March 2023

68895821R10105